The Girl in the Red Bonnet

A Christmas Story

by

Cliff Miles

This book is a work of fiction. Names, characters, places, and incidents either are imaginary or are used fictitiously, and any resemblance to actual persons, living or dead, events, or locales is entirely coincidence.

ISBN 978-0-8425-2984-6

Acknowledgements

My wife, Natalie, has been my number one supporter throughout the entire process of creating this book—so much so that she designed the copy that you now hold in your hands and saw it through to its publication online as well.

Natalie recommended that I approach Lena Harper to edit the book, which proved to be sage advice. Lena provided two comprehensive edits that improved the book immensely. She showed me that I can tell a story, "just" not write it.

Much thanks to Judy Garvin, who provided an early edit and made suggestions that I incorporated into the narrative.

My daughter Vanessa Miles Adams was the first to read my first draft, and she was the first to read the final draft. Fortunately for me, she found many corrections. I remain hopeful that you, dear reader, will not discover any more, but I won't hold my breath. I know how I write.

The bottom line is that I am grateful to all the women who helped me make this book what it is.

Author's Note

I love the name Natalie; I always have. I heard it for the very first time when I met a young woman I liked from the moment I saw her. As she approached I said, "Hi, my name's Cliff. What's yours?"

She answered, "Natalie."

I have been chasing Natalie ever since. I love her; she is my wife of thirty-four years and hopefully thirty-four more. I wanted to use Natalie's name for the main character to honor her. When I learned the meaning of her name, I was delighted. *Natalie,* Latin for "Christmas Day." It was lovely finding that out. Destiny, maybe?

It has been my desire for some time to write a Christmas story. The idea came to me as a whisper on November 22, 2013, and since it was presented to me, I was compelled to write it.

Prologue

A loud pop rang through the still air, falling on deaf ears. The frozen river began crazing, cracking, and splitting under the prostrate body of the girl. Moments later the ice lost the struggle to support her, and she was gone.

Part One

Every now and then a child is born who becomes someone everyone naturally loves. Natalie Cooper was just such a person.

1858
The Nathan Cooper Grist Mill

Nathan Cooper bought a mill, and then he built a family. The mill, with its sixteen-foot waterwheel and its forty-eight buckets, turned two sets of stones for a total production of four hundred pounds of flour per hour. This mill was very special because its waterwheel never stopped turning. One of the conditions of Mr. Cooper's purchase was that he would never let the waterwheel stop, because legend had it that if it stopped, so would the world. Just like his predecessors, he took this tale seriously and performed maintenance at the appointed times—during the full moons of summer. Thus, the good people of Chester never knew of a time when the waterwheel was not in constant motion. They were proud citizens knowing that they had a hand in keeping the world going.

The world hasn't stopped, so you can be sure that the Nathan Cooper grist mill is still in motion to this very day.

Now, Chester is in Morris County, New Jersey, a place known for being the northernmost part of the country where Christmas mistletoe can be found. Chester was an important crossroads for travelers passing through the area and had everything that one would need. Parker and Olsen had the carriage works. The blacksmith shop was owned by the Parmer brothers. Two Sisters Cider Mill was now owned by only one sister, Miss Nicole Koch. The largest buildings were Henry Livingston's Sawmill and the Westmore Hotel. Mrs. Adams's General Store was its heart, and the little white church, presided over by Bishop Brian Versey, was its soul. And just out of town stood Nathan Cooper's grist mill.

The mill's waterwheel—turning year after year, day after day, minute after minute—had now counted six years, seven months, one week, and one day since Mr. Cooper's daughter Natalie was born in the year of our Lord 1864. A tiny bundle with lots of brunette hair, she came as an early morning Christmas gift to Mr. Cooper and his wife, Clarice.

As a child Natalie was in no way exceptional. She was just a pretty little girl who liked playing with her dolls, being outdoors, and finding interesting things to bring home. She was a little sister to Benjamin and later a big sister to Christelle. She would help if asked and was very fond of reading. As she grew she learned how to stand her ground, which was a rare trait for a young lady in the 1870's.

June 1873
Mrs. Messing

Eight-year-old Natalie Cooper met Mrs. Viola Messing in a most unfortunate way. She practically ran her over while hurrying out of Mrs. Linden's ladies store, anxious to show her father her very first store-bought dress. This near collision caused Mrs. Messing to speak sternly at the retreating Natalie.

"Young lady—if that's what you are—stop this instant," she commanded.

Natalie stopped and turned to find herself face to face with a tiny wisp of a woman who smelled like lilacs. Her gray hair was put up in a bun so tight that it was hard to tell that it was hair and not a hat.

"Are you going to apologize?" she demanded.

"Yes, ma'am. I'm sorry," uttered Natalie.

"Sorry for what?"

"I'm sorry that I almost ran you over."

"Almost? You most certainly did run me over. I'm lucky that I'm not all broken up! I can still feel where you struck me, and I don't hesitate to tell you that I bruise easily. Tomorrow I am going to have bruises the size of baseballs, I can assure you."

"I've never seen a bruise anywhere near that size," stated Natalie.

"Are you questioning my integrity for telling the truth?" demanded Mrs. Messing.

"Oh, no ma'am. It's that I've never seen bruises like that, and if you do happen to get one—which I hope you don't— I would very much like to see it."

"Why on earth do you want to see my bruises?"

"To kiss them all better," she said without hesitation.

This took Mrs. Messing by surprise, so much so that it was a few moments before she answered. "To kiss them all better?" she said, her voice rising. "No one ever kisses m . . . I have not been kissed by anyone in more than fifty-five years," she stated flatly. Unpleasant memories invaded from Mrs. Messing's past, of the time when she had been kissed—and proposed to. She had accepted, but she had foolishly left her fiancé because in her youthful ignorance she found him want-ing. She had lived alone ever since. Being forced to remember this really got her dander up, so she changed the subject and verbally attacked the girl.

"Well, my fine pretty little peacock, I can think of at least half a dozen etiquette rules that you have broken since you assaulted me. If one desires to be a lady, walk like a lady. Do not dress in bright and gaudy colors to attract attention—and that red dress of yours certainly does attract attention. A lady should wear gloves at all times, even when shaking hands. You have no gloves. Don't make noises with your hands or feet. And don't crowd people or bump elbows," she concluded.

"That's only five," stated Natalie.

"Don't be flippant with me, young lady."

"I'm not. You said that you could think of at least half a dozen and you only told me five that I have broken. What about the sixth?"

Mrs. Messing was unaccustomed to being challenged, and she never let a challenge go unanswered. This girl had spunk and she liked spunk. However, she would never tell her so. This girl needed to be shown her place, and show her her place she would! "Number six: ladies may walk unattended on the street, being careful to neither walk with a hurried step, stand in front of shop windows and stare in, look backward, nor send notice to anyone who ventures to address them. Be sure that you get home before dark, and do not be out after dusk. You, young lady, you were walking with much more than a hurried step."

"Number six certainly has a lot to it," Natalie said, impressed.

"There are many more. I can recite nearly a hundred rules of etiquette, and any proper girl worth her salt would already know them."

"I have never heard of them," said Natalie.

"You've never heard of *any* of them?" This gave Mrs. Messing pause to the point that she had to consider what to say. "I am getting the feeling that you have not been brought up in a proper home. Don't they teach you any manners?"

"My mama did teach me what politeness is: skillful management of our words and actions, whereby we make other people have a better opinion of us and themselves," she said, meeting Mrs. Messing's eyes.

"Well I never," replied Mrs. Messing, stung by Natalie's inference. "What is your name, young lady?"

"Natalie Cooper, ma'am."

"I am going to have a talk with your mother and let her know just what kind of daughter she has, and I will be sure to make suggestions for your improvement."

"She's in Mrs. Linden's ladies store shopping for herself. I'm off to show my father my dress," whereupon Natalie walked away, not wanting to upset this woman any more than she already had. Some distance away, Natalie thought to herself that she didn't need any improvement from this woman who hadn't properly introduced herself. She would come to know Mrs. Messing as hard-bitten and curt with everyone who knew her.

Mrs. Messing walked straight into Mrs. Linden's ladies store quite upset at having been slighted.

December 1873
The Red Bonnet
Around the time of Natalie's ninth Christmas, her mother made her a beautiful red bonnet. Natalie loved it, and because she had received it at Christmastime, it became her official Christmas symbol. She wore it as soon as the Christmas season began, and she wore it whenever she was on official Christmas business. Wearing it reminded her of what she was about and for whom. Almost everyone in town knew how special that red bonnet was.

From her mother Natalie learned very early the association of her name to the day she was born, and she made it her mission to make Christmas special for everyone, especially her brother, Benjamin. On December 25 it was a Cooper family tradition to celebrate Christmas in the morning and Natalie's birthday later that day. Natalie was always prepared with thoughtful gifts for him so he wouldn't feel left out. Benjamin, however, was not bothered in the least that she received more attention. In fact, he was wholly pleased, for they were able to celebrate his little sister's birthday on the same day that they celebrated the Savior's.

Most years he received at least two things from her: something to wear and something to eat. When she was younger the something to eat came from the General Store and the something to wear had their mother's touch. As Natalie grew in skills as well as years, Benjamin took ever more delight in her artful creations. His favorite was his scarf of many colors.

December 1874
Christmas

On her tenth Christmas, Natalie surprised everyone and changed her tradition. Instead of something bought from a store, she gave Benjamin a letter, writing it as if it had come from the Savior, telling Benjamin how and what he wanted him to be.

Dear Benjamin,

My Christmas wish for you this coming year is that you will continue to grow big and strong so that you can watch over your little sister, so that you will be able to help your mama and papa with happiness in your heart, and so that you will always remember me and the gifts I have given you. But most of all I want you to be grateful and to have joy in your heart.
Love to you from me.

Benjamin was deeply touched. The beautiful spirit of the letter added to the loving bond between him and his sister. The next Christmas, everyone in the Cooper household followed Natalie's example and wrote letters to one another as if they had come from the Savior. After a while, giving two gifts—one carefully made and one tenderly written—became the tradition in the Cooper home.

One little touch that Natalie had written, "Love to you from me," was continued. The Cooper family always signed their letters on behalf of the Savior, and "Love to you from me" always made the Cooper family feel closer to him at Christmastime. The letters were saved, and over time they became the most precious of gifts.

Nathan Cooper was dark-haired, square-jawed, of average height, and extremely strong from lifting hundredweights of flour day after day. He was kind and patient with his wife and children—and with everyone he met. An only child, he would usually defer to Mrs. Cooper regarding the children. When it came to hunting and fishing, however, Mr. Cooper was in charge of Benjamin's learning, and the two of them spent many a happy hour together in the nearby forest and along the river.

Clarice Cooper was French and very proud of it. She was a serene woman but firm in the way that she wanted things done—especially with regard to taking care of the house and the children. The eldest of seven children, she had helped to raise her five sisters and one brother. She and Natalie kept their lovely home shining.

Sixteen-year-old Benjamin, named after Mr. Franklin, was already a reflection of his father. There was usually a twinkle in his hazel eyes. He was a responsible boy, always looking out for Natalie and making sure no harm came to her, such as falling in the river when he took her fishing or falling out of trees when he taught her how to climb. He helped his father as often as needed and had another job delivering goods to the outer farms for Mrs. Adams, who owned the General Store.

Overall the Nathan Cooper household was untroubled and in good spirits.

September 1875 (Natalie Is 10)
Questions

Natalie Cooper watched her mother's anguished face, wondering if she should bother her. But she wanted answers, so got up the nerve to ask.

"Mama, what's wrong with Benny?" inquired Natalie with concern.

"I don't know. He started to feel ill while he and Herman were on deliveries today, and now he has a fever and is quite sick."

"Are you going for the doctor?"

"Father has already gone for him."

"I hope Benny's going to be okay. Can I go see him?"

"No. If it's something catching, I don't want you to get it. You're going to have to send him notes if you want to tell him anything—and no sneaking into his room while I'm not around! You understand?"

"Yes, I understand. I want to write him and let him know that I am thinking of him and that I want him to get well soon."

"I think he would like that very much."

With that Natalie went to get paper and a pen.

❄ ❄ ❄

Mr. and Mrs. Cooper met the doctor the moment he came out of Benjamin's room.

"I've done all I can for now, Mr. and Mrs. Cooper," said Dr. Anderson. It's up to Benjamin's constitution as to whether or not he will get well. Because he has been healthy and strong, I have high hope for his recovery."

"Oh, I do hope you are right! Do you know what he has?" asked Mrs. Cooper.

"Looks like influenza to me, but I can't be sure. Just in case it might be wise to limit visitors."

"Thank you Dr. Anderson," replied Mr. Cooper. "I will see you to your buggy."

❄ ❄ ❄

Mrs. Cooper kept a constant vigil at Benjamin's bedside, tirelessly caring for him. Before dawn on the fifth morning, she rose stiffly from her old blue rocking chair to again check on her son. He was still very pale, but his skin was cool to the touch, and he appeared to be sleeping peacefully. Encouraged, she decided to sleep in her own bed for a few hours before preparing breakfast for the family.

Warm rays of sunlight awakened Mrs. Cooper and, with the hope that a new day brings, she returned to Benjamin's room only to find her son cold in death. The shock pierced her heart. With trembling hands she gently brushed his hair from his eyes, tears blinding her own.

"Oh God, no!" she wailed, looking heavenward. "Not this. Not this. He was getting better. This cannot happen! We need him here. We need him here with us, not with you!"

She then lay her head over Benjamin's still heart, gave in to her grief, and released the sobs welling up from her soul. Her last act before leaving the room was to kiss her son on the cheek, already missing him terribly.

❄ ❄ ❄

Benjamin's death marked the moment that Natalie started to become someone who everyone came to love.

Over the ensuing days, she became confused as to why her brother had been taken from the family. "It just doesn't seem fair. Why not someone else?" she asked herself. At once she felt remorse that she should wish such pain on anyone else, but muddled thoughts were swimming through her mind, so she urgently sought out her mother. She found her in the kitchen making bread to distract herself. It looked to Natalie as if there was going to be enough bread to last a month.

"Mama, why was Benny taken to heaven?"

Mrs. Cooper, startled, froze in her dough. She still felt so raw from the loss of her son that she could hardly breath, hardly think. Making bread, which had always come naturally, was now a monumental task. Why she had started making the bread she didn't even know. Natalie's question should not have surprised her. It was the one burning in her own heart for which she had no answer. She knew she must say something, so she decided to give the simplest answer she could with the hope that it would satisfy her daughter. However, she knew more questions would follow.

"I don't know, dear. Sometimes people just die, and often there are no answers why."

"Will I die?"

Though unobserved by Natalie, the question caused Mrs. Cooper's fingers to tear through the loaf of bread that she was forming but her voice remained calm. "We all die, but, the Lord willing, you won't for a very, very long time."

"Mama, I could die tomorrow, couldn't I?" Natalie ventured.

"Don't say th . . ." Mrs. Cooper caught herself, forcing down the unsaid words. She started to reform her ruined loaf of bread while regaining her composure. She said quietly, "Yes, it is possible, but very unlikely."

"Why?"

"Because you are a healthy, happy, growing young lady, and for most people in your situation, it just doesn't happen."

"But it does for some?" persisted Natalie.

"Yes, it does for some!"

Realizing that the questions were becoming too painful for her mother, Natalie left her remaining questions unasked. "Thank you, Mama," she whispered as she withdrew from the kitchen, leaving her mother alone again to bake life-giving bread in an effort to soothe the pain of death.

For many days Natalie pondered what she had been told. She stayed quiet and inside herself, interested only in her own thoughts. During one afternoon, lost in contemplation, Natalie reasoned, "Someday I am going to die. It could be on any day. I have no idea how many more days I have, so I had better make the most of them."

At a very young age Natalie had discovered her mortality.

October 17, 1875
Voyage
Nathan Cooper had made up his mind. He would tell his wife and daughter of his decision once Natalie made it down for breakfast.

"Do you think Natalie will be long in coming?" he asked his wife casually.

"Not long, I should think. I heard her stirring and told her that hot cakes would be for breakfast. You know how much she loves them," she replied, while flipping three hot cakes onto a plate for her husband.

"That should have had her here before sunup. Should I go see what she's about?"

"No, no, that won't be necessary. She is still having very dark times with the loss of Benjamin, as am I."

This comment only confirmed to Mr. Cooper that he was doing the right thing.

Natalie came in looking rather haggard. She touched her father on the shoulder. With a faint smile she greeted her parents. "Good morning, Papa—Mama."

Her father patted her hand. "Did you sleep?"

"I don't really know. I had bad dreams, and when I wasn't having bad dreams I was thinking about Benny, and it all just got jumbled together."

Mrs. Cooper presented Natalie with hot cakes and eggs, which brought a little life to her face.

Mr. Cooper decided the time was right to present his idea. "I have given what I am about to say a great deal of thought. We are not thriving as a family right now, so I have decided to do something about it. Clarice, my sweet wife, I am sending you and Natalie to visit your family in France. I think that a change of scenery would do you both a great deal of good. I myself can't go with you because of my responsibilities at the mill, though I sincerely wish I could. I will miss you terribly."

Natalie looked up in surprise and with some anxiety. She had never traveled overseas. Questioning eyes met her mother's, but she said nothing, waiting for her mother's response.

Mrs. Cooper was about to object, but she could see that it would be futile. Her husband had said that he had already given the matter, "a great deal of thought." She had learned over the years that when he used that particular phrase, it would be easier moving mountains.

"As you wish, Nathan. When do you suppose we should leave?"

"As soon as you can. I will make inquires later today."

❊ ❊ ❊

With cables sent and arrangements made, the trip to Bordeaux, France, began on October 22 aboard the steamship *Frisia*. Natalie and Mrs. Cooper would embark from New York, relieved to take this particular ship because Mr. Cooper had informed them it was proven to be one of the better steamships—fast and very well built. They would be on the Atlantic Ocean for only eleven days. Natalie wore her red bonnet on the day that they boarded because the excitement of the occasion made her feel like it was Christmas.

The S. S. *Frisia* was a black beast of a ship. From where Natalie stood on the dock, it loomed frightfully large. While boarding, Natalie caught sight of a man who was very smartly dressed, and she knew he must be the captain. As she was taking in all of the pretty accoutrements on his uniform, he caught her admiring them. Smiling, he tipped his cap at her and nodded. Embarrassed that she had been noticed, she quickly turned her gaze to other parts of the ship and was surprised to notice small masts for sails. To her eye they didn't look very useful for such a large ship. Natalie counted ten metallic lifeboats, all secure and ready for disaster. She hoped they would never need to be used. One-way stairways connected the decks so that there would be no unpleasant meetings between the upward- and downward-bound passengers.

❋ ❋ ❋

Natalie and her mother were shown to their stateroom, which was, in Natalie's estimation, about eight by ten feet. It was well furnished and nicely ornamented. After settling in, she and her mother continued to explore the ship. They discovered salons, conversation rooms, and smoking rooms that were beautifully finished with bird's-eye maple panels and trimmed in mahogany. Pretty little accent ornaments and gilded figure-work finished off the décor. The ladies' sitting room on the upper deck was their favorite with all its beautiful furniture. A purser told them it had been designed for female passengers to use during unpleasant weather. Natalie and her mother agreed the room was a desirable addition to the ship's conveniences.

Though her excitement for the ship to get underway was growing, Natalie was already missing home—even if the ship now appeared a little less ominous.

Soon after the ship left port, Natalie began to feel ill. Her mother took her back to their stateroom in case it was something serious. As Natalie grew worse, Mrs. Cooper realized that her daughter's malady was seasickness. When Mrs. Cooper first came to America twenty years earlier, she had seen other passengers with seasickness and knew it should soon pass.

Each morning Mrs. Cooper hoped that Natalie would be better, but she was not. Mrs. Cooper couldn't understand why Natalie wasn't improving, but she persisted in thinking that no one could take better care of her daughter than she could. It was only seasickness after all—not an actual illness. Because of Mrs. Cooper's stubbornness Natalie suffered terribly for the entire voyage.

❄ ❄ ❄

When they arrived in Bordeaux, they were relieved to step onto solid ground and into the comforts of Mrs. Cooper's family's home. However, though Natalie's relatives were ever so kind and tried to make her happy, over the ensuing days deep homesickness crept over her. She felt displaced—lost with the language, awkward with the customs, and uncomfortable around all these people that she didn't know. Each day away from home Natalie grew a little darker.

While in Bordeaux Mrs. Cooper learned that her Grandmother Rolland was in poor health and that if she ever wanted to see her again, it would need to be during this trip. Visiting Grandmother Rolland required a train ride to Paris, which proved to be a pleasant distraction for Natalie.

About midway through the journey, Natalie and her mother went to the dining car. Two men seated across the aisle from them were deep in conversation, and Mrs. Cooper, overhearing them, told Natalie that one of them was a sculptor and that they were on their way to Paris to raise money for a statue.

Natalie guessed that the sculptor was the animated man with wavy brown hair and a beard and mustache. So absorbed in his discussion was he that he failed to notice when he brushed a sheet of paper from the table. The paper floated across the aisle and came to rest at Natalie's feet. Without hesitation, Natalie picked it up, got up from her table, and carefully set it on the table of the two men. Glancing down at the drawing, she saw it was of a very large hand holding a torch. On the table there were other drawings of the statue, and she could see that they were of a woman holding a torch.

Natalie returned to her seat and told her mother what she had seen. While they were having dinner, Mrs. Cooper continued to overhear bits of dialogue between the two men and learned that the statue was to go to New York.

"Mama, did you say that they are going to Paris to raise money?"

"Yes, I am sure that is what they are doing."

"May I give them something?"

"Why?"

"The drawings—they are very beautiful, and I want to help if the statue is to come to America."

This was the first time Natalie had shown any interest in anything since they had come to France. Mrs. Cooper considered the request for only a moment before handing her ten francs. Natalie got up when she noticed the men were about to leave. She tugged on the coat of the man she supposed to be the sculptor.

He said in French, "Yes, miss, what is it?"

Natalie turned to her mother for help, and Mrs. Cooper explained in her native French what Natalie wanted to do.

The man introduced himself as Mr. Frederic Auguste Bartholdi and asked, "You are American?"

Natalie understood the word and nodded her head affirmatively.

"I accept your very kind gift on behalf of the French people," he continued in English. "You, young lady, are the very first American to give for the statue." He accepted her money. Then he produced a little notebook, asked her name, and wrote down, "Miss Natalie Cooper of Chester, New

Jersey: **10** francs." He showed her what he had written, got down on one knee, and kissed her on both cheeks.

"Thank you very much. May God bless you, Natalie."

The other man nodded to both of them as they left the dining car. Natalie, feeling a little happier, smiled at her mother.

❄ ❄ ❄

It was in Paris that a most extraordinary thing happened. After a tender visit with her grandmother, Mrs. Cooper took Natalie on a stroll down the Champs-Élysées to show her where she had spent summers as a child and to revisit childhood memories.

On the walk they passed a few artists who were taking advantage of the warm fall day. Natalie was only along to humor her mother. Thus far nothing about Paris interested her. It was just a tremendously big city that smelled bad.

Suddenly Natalie stopped to observe a young man in his early twenties using paints that really intrigued her. The colors on the heavy white paper were rich and yet transparent. She watched in awe as he laid down colors, all the while being instructed, by another man who was wearing a dark graying beard and mustache. Natalie watched so long that the artist stopped and introduced himself as Jean-Francois Raffaelli.

"What kind of paints are those?" Natalie ventured to ask. Her mother translated for her and Jean-Francois responded that they were watercolors.

"Have you ever made a painting?" he asked.

Natalie looked to her mother for the translation and then shook her head no. He set his painting aside, produced another paper, and had her sit on his lap. Her mother continued to translate.

"Look out there on the street," he said pointing, "and draw what you see. Just a few lines to suggest something to you."

With a few strokes she had what she wanted. This got the attention of both men.

Raffaelli turned to Mrs. Cooper. "Mademoiselle, does she know art? This is very good."

"No, monsieur," replied Mrs. Cooper.

He turned his attention back to Natalie. "Let us see what you can do with paint."

Natalie held the brush in the same way that she had seen Monsieur Raffaelli hold it and started with the faintest blues to create the November sky that she saw before her. She worked the painting from back to front and light to dark, adding all of the things that she felt needed to be there to create just the right balance. As Natalie painted, Monsieur Raffaelli made encouraging and satisfactory noises that she understood to mean she was doing well.

As this impromptu lesson was unfolding, the older man kept looking at Natalie. He moved about to see her at various angles, all the while talking to her mother with an accent that didn't sound very French to Natalie's ears.

It took only a short while for Natalie to produce what she wanted, and when she was finished she had captured a little piece of Paris with barren trees, buggies, a few people, and, off in the distance the Arc de Triomphe. Inside she was pleased.

Monsieur Raffaelli spoke to Mrs. Cooper. "You should see to it that she learns the art."

He had Natalie sign her painting in the lower right corner. "A little piece of magic, yes?" he said, presenting it to her.

Natalie nodded, smiling at her results.

The other man was then introduced as Monsieur Alexei Harlamoff. He asked Mrs. Cooper, "How long are you to be in Paris?"

"I don't know," she replied. "A few more days perhaps."

"Would you please permit me to paint your daughter?"

Before Mrs. Cooper could respond, Monsieur Raffaelli informed her that Monsieur Harlamoff was a Russian artist, who was very well known for his portraits. She should find it an honor that he would make time to paint her daughter, especially because he was about to start a commission of Pauline Viardot, who was a very famous opera singer, and that painting would be delayed.

Mrs. Cooper asked Monsieur Harlamoff, "How much time would you need?"

He started to reply and then reconsidered, realizing that he didn't want to lose the chance to paint this beautifully sad little girl. "Three days, madam. I will work very fast, and I promise that you will have a painting that will be around much longer than I."

Mrs. Cooper considered the offer. It would be something else to do, and Natalie would get a chance to see how another artist worked. Maybe, just maybe, she would come out of her darkness.

"I accept your kind offer. It will cost how much?"

"Nothing! I want to do this. I want to try and capture her . . . her inner soul, if I can."

Arrangements were made, and the next day Natalie sat for the artist. They arrived at the address they had been given, with Natalie wearing her red bonnet, not because she was on any Christmas errand but because the day had turned raw and cold.

When Monsieur Harlamoff saw her wearing it, He was so taken with the little brown haired girl in the red bonnet that he insisted that she wear it for the painting. He sketched her first, and soon there was another Natalie in the room— only this time she was a whisper of lines on the large, white canvas. What Mrs. Cooper could see in the drawing gave her prickles all over her skin. Monsieur Harlamoff was pleased.

In his broken French he said, "Even now I see it coming under my fingers."

Monsieur Harlamoff spent the majority of the time working on just her eyes. His whole countenance was aflame with the soul of an artist who is seeing his vision appear before him on the canvas.

At the end of each day Natalie walked over to the painting and examined the progress of her twin. This painting was going to haunt her whenever she looked at it, reminding her that the girl in the painting was mourning the loss of Benny. However, she did not want to dampen her mother's excitement, so she chose not to share her feelings and only smiled and nodded when asked what she thought of it.

At the end of the sittings, Monsieur Harlamoff had completed her face and had partially blocked in the remaining part of the painting to the point where any observer would have an idea of what to expect when it was finished. He told Mrs. Cooper that he would complete the painting later and then have it sent to them in America.

❄ ❄ ❄

Mrs. Cooper and Natalie received the finished painting some months later along with a letter from Monsieur Harlamoff.

*I apologize for having taken so long, but when I saw the results of what we had done, I took the liberty of painting another copy for myself. Both paintings are nearly identical. You have the canvas that I originally produced. I do hope you like it. The copy has already become much loved by my friends, and I have already turned down **10,000** francs for it. I intend to keep it.*

Sincerely, Alexei Alexeievich Harlamoff

P.S. Should you and your lovely daughter get back to Paris, I would like to see you both.

P.P.S. I almost forgot, the enclosed watercolors are a gift from Monsieur Raffaelli. He says to make sure that you "get her the art lessons."

It was such a lovely painting, and it captured perfectly the way that Natalie had been feeling in Paris. Monsieur Harlamoff had taken only one liberty that the Coopers could see, and that was to make Natalie's hair longer than it actually was. The addition of the hair in little waves added an untidy prettiness to the child in the painting. The final touch of genius was the way he left the bonnet not quite finished, which drove their eyes to Natalie's face. The painting was magically lovely and yet sad.

Mr. Cooper treasured it, and for quite some time it brought tears to his eyes—so much so that each time he saw it he felt it necessary to find Natalie to give her a warm embrace and a kiss on the forehead.

❄ ❄ ❄

The time in France was a healing balm for Mrs. Cooper. She would like to have stayed longer, but Natalie was not thriving and needed to be taken home as soon as possible. Natalie was even willing to suffer through another bout of her nightmare of seasickness just to get home.

December 2, 1875
Heading for Home, Day 1
They left Bordeaux on a quiet, cool morning. Natalie stood beside her mother staring up at the hull of the S. S. *Frisia,* trepidation growing with each moment as memories of the first voyage returned. It was stifling. The same ship—likely the same nightmares. If it hadn't been the only way to get home, she would not have stepped foot on it. Before boarding in New York she was excited for her first trip across the ocean.

Now she knew exactly what ocean travel meant for her: a hell that had to be endured if she were going to get home.

Natalie froze and pulled back as their turn to board approached.

Taking Natalie's hand, Mrs. Cooper tenderly coaxed her along. "I know. We will just have to make the best of it. I hope for your sake that you will be better this time. I will do my best to make you as comfortable as possible, and this time I will get whatever help I can for you. There must be a way to help you. Now we need to get on board."

Quiet tears accompanied Natalie as she walked onto the ship.

Natalie and her mother lingered on deck as the S. S. *Frisia* sailed leisurely down the Gironde River, through the estuary, and out into the Bay of Biscay.

"Mama, look at those three sailing ships! They are so small!"

Mrs. Cooper pointed out the Cordouan Lighthouse. "It is hundreds of years old and one of the tallest lighthouses in the world."

"It looks like an upside-down torch," observed Natalie. "Remember the torch held by the Lady Liberty statue in Monsieur Bartholdi's drawings?"

Mrs. Cooper tipped her head to get a better look. "Yes, I suppose it does," she agreed.

After emerging into the French Atlantic, the four ships headed for different points of the compass, with the S. S. *Frisia* heading due west. The wind was gently blowing, and the sea was almost at a dead calm, for which Natalie was grateful. All that morning and throughout the day they glided over the still waters.

They met Mrs. Etheridge while they were out on deck taking in the sunset. Overhearing another passenger's comments on seasickness, Mrs. Etheridge declared, "I believe in fooling yourself. Whenever I feel it coming on, I stand in front of the mirror and repeat three times, 'I don't get seasick.' And make sure you say it with conviction. It works for me."

Natalie decided she would try it the moment she was back in their stateroom after dinner. Approaching their room with her mother, she felt her worst fears coming on.

"Mama, where is your mirror, please?" she asked with urgency. Mrs. Cooper retrieved her small hand mirror and gave it to Natalie. Repeating Mrs. Etheridge's instructions with conviction, she prayed that it would work.

It didn't. The discordance to Natalie's mind sent her whole body into a general state of alarm. She was bedridden shortly thereafter, and closing her eyes helped ever so little. As before, she tried concentrating on the inner surroundings of the ship, hoping against hope that she might have become a little stronger since their voyage over, but she was now fully seasick, and her dinner was lost shortly thereafter. The only thing that eased her discomfort was sleep. The only problem was that she couldn't sleep twenty-four hours a day.

With concern and determination, Mrs. Cooper told Natalie, "I am going to go and talk to someone about this and see if they can help. I'll be back as soon as I can."

Natalie, already too sick to care, didn't respond. Before too long Mrs. Cooper returned with a purser carrying a pan of ice water.

While he placed the pan on the floor he explained to Natalie how some sailors had told him that putting your feet in ice water helped. "It works for some, miss. I swear by it. Let's get you up and give it a try."

Mrs. Cooper removed Natalie's stockings and placed her feet in the icy water.

For Natalie the cold was a welcome distraction from her nausea. However, she was quickly trading one misery for another. She stood the ice water for as long as she possibly could, hoping for relief. Additional spasms gave her the answer. She removed her feet and collapsed back onto her bed.

Mrs. Cooper attended to drying her feet, and the unhappy purser took his leave of them. "I am deeply sorry, madam," he said as he closed the door behind him.

December 3 and 4, 1875
Days 2 and 3

Purser Sam Swain was always harried and beset by a hundred cares and little miseries of other people. In spite of this he always presented an unfailing front of courtesy—smiling and going cheerily about his duties. How he did this day after day, month after month, year after year, no one knew. After escorting Mrs. Cooper back to her stateroom from the ladies sitting room, he spotted the little girl propped up in the corner of her bed, looking dreadful. He had seen it hundreds of times before, and hundreds of times he had used the same lines to get his charges up and out on the deck. Sometimes it actually made a difference. His job was to provide hope.

"Sea air is a tonic that courses like an elixir in your blood, miss, especially with you young women. How about we get you up on deck all bundled up. I'm sure it will do you some good. Shall we give it a try? I will hand you directly to Mr. Kruger, and he will see to it that you are well taken care of. Will that suit you, miss?"

Natalie looked at her mother, not knowing what to say. Mrs. Cooper hesitated and then nodded. Natalie turned to the purser and said, "Yes, thank you," in a very little voice.

Deck Steward Kruger was of a similar bent. Whether the wind was blowing high or low, in fair weather or foul, he was ever the same—bright, beaming, optimistic, and encouraging. He was especially sympathetic to those who suffered from seasickness.

"Mr. Kruger, this is Miss Cooper. She is quite green around the gills, and I expect you to take good care of her and return her back to me with a more natural color. Do you think you can do it?"

"I'll give it my best, Mr. Swain."

"I know you will," Sam responded cheerily, handing Natalie off.

Taking Natalie by the arm, Mr. Kruger helped Mrs. Cooper escort her daughter directly to mid-ship.

"This is the best place on the whole of the ship while up on my deck," he said. "The middle here moves the least. Now, if you have to get up and heave, do it to leeward."

Natalie, looked at Mr. Kruger with questioning eyes. "Downwind, miss," he explained. "That way it won't come back on you—understand?"

Natalie nodded ever so slightly, not wanting to give her head a reason to signal her stomach to react. She currently had no desire to experience heaving to leeward.

Once he had Mrs. Cooper and Natalie all settled in deck chairs, he said, "I'll see you momentarily," and left to attend others in his charge.

Carefully looking around, Natalie noticed that the center of the ship was occupied by others, some looking just as grim as she felt. Remembering being told that watching others become seasick was contagious, she quickly looked to her mother for comfort.

Natalie spent the remainder of the day sleeping, and when it was time to leave for the night, she wasn't happy to have to get up, but the rules of the ship didn't allow passengers to sleep on deck. Though still terribly sick, she had managed to keep everything down.

Day three was nearly identical to the previous, with the exception that at the end of the day Mr. Kruger had one more bit of help to provide. He said, "I know you young ones like the sweets, but avoid them if you can, miss. Surely they will make you light headed and dizzy and even more miserable than you already are." Natalie couldn't possibly see how she could be more miserable than she already was.

December 5, 1875
Day 4

The ship moved on through the great waters, indifferent to its surroundings. The people on board, however, awoke to a rare surprise: it was snowing! By the time breakfast was over, there were three inches of snow on deck, and more was coming down. Everything was dusted in white, and visibility was less than the length of the ship. While some on board looked at the snow with amusement, others were not at all pleased with the situation, looking at it as an inconvenience and another hazard, since the decks had become slippery. For Natalie it was just another element added to her seasickness to be tolerated while she was on board a ship that couldn't get to New York fast enough. All she wanted was to get to solid ground.

December 6, 1875
Day 5

Once again Natalie awoke to her misery, fighting to get back to sleep. Her stomach would not let her. It was empty for want of food and at the same time was intent on rejecting anything that was put inside it. Her mother was not to be seen, and this caused her some distress.

Natalie had just about decided to go and look for her when Mrs. Cooper entered their stateroom carrying a tray. "I have a hot tea for you," she declared. "I met a woman at breakfast who told me that ginger tea works for some with seasickness. It is a favorite remedy that has worked for enough passengers that they now keep an ample supply. I hope it helps."

Natalie managed to sit up as her mother brought the warm tea to her lips. It was unexpectedly not sweet. Then she remembered that Mr. Kruger had said that sweets would not do well in her stomach. The smell was wonderful and its warmth was welcome, and for the moment the tea was staying down.

"Well?" asked her mother. "Is it going to stay down?"

"I think so," replied Natalie.

"Do you want the rest?"

"Yes, please."

This was the first relief that Natalie had had since she had come on board. This respite lasted for only a short while, but the tea had helped. Natalie spent the rest of the day in bed trying to sleep. She was spared having to use her bucket.

December 7 and 8, 1875
Days 6 And 7

After another round of ginger tea, Natalie wanted to leave her stateroom again for as long as possible. The ship was in relatively calm seas, so she was intent on giving it a go. She and her mother met Mr. and Mrs. Hamblin at breakfast. They were returning home to Maine after visiting relatives in England and touring in France.

Mrs. Hamblin could see that Natalie was suffering and let her know what had worked for her own seasickness. "An old sailing myth is that when the sea gets rough, eat only saltines. Old salts swear by it. Helps me in the mornings." She continued, "I also found that they helped when I was with child. I would eat a few first thing in the morning and then I could make it through the rest of the day."

Natalie was grateful for the advice and decided that her mother should obtain some crackers.

The first thing that next morning Natalie reached for and found the saltines that had been placed near her pillow. She ate only four, not wanting to waste them should they come back up on her. She was pleased to find that they helped. Her stomach was a little satisfied, and they were staying down for the moment.

December 9, 1875
Day 8

A knock on the stateroom door brought Mrs. Cooper face to face with a nice-looking young man who called himself Mr. Halvorsen. He came in carrying a small bundle.

"I have been instructed by Mr. Swain to bring this for you. We are going to set it up in the hope that you will have better nights." The young man produced an object that Natalie had never seen before. "What is it?" she asked.

"A hammock," he replied. "Strung fore-to-aft, it will let you lie motionless while the ship rolls beneath you. You will still feel the up-and-down heave of the ship, but it does reduce the rolls and should help you sleep better."

It did!

December 10, 1875
Day 9

Natalie decided that she wanted to try and get some fresh air, walk a little, and see if she could find her "sea legs." The hammock had given her the best night's sleep in days, and the saltines and ginger tea were staying down.

"Mama, you look nearly worn out from taking care of me. Stay here and sleep. I am confident that I'll be fine."

"Are you sure, Natalie?"

"Yes, and if I start to get sick I will make my way back quickly." Whereupon Natalie went over to her mother and gave her a kiss on the cheek.

Natalie saw two men playing a game that she had always wanted to learn: chess. She watched them play for as long as she could, finding the moves mystifying. The older of the two introduced himself as Mr. Charles C. Miles and his son, as Clark. She learned that they were from England and were on their way to the United States to visit family in Indiana. They were very kind and took time to show her the basic moves of the game pieces.

"Father wins most of the time," Clark said, "but every now and then I manage to sneak in a victory."

"He's getting better all the time, and it's not going to be for much longer that I will have the advantage," replied Mr. Miles.

"Father and I like to play from early afternoon until the lights are turned out. It really helps to pass the time."

Watching the game had temporarily distracted Natalie from feeling ill, but nausea was now overcoming her again. She would have fallen off her chair if Clark had not caught her just in time.

"Are you ill?" he asked.

"Seasickness—the whole voyage," she replied

"Let's get you back to your room so that you can lie down." Whereupon the Miles gentlemen suspended their game and took Natalie back to her mother.

After introductions the elder Mr. Miles said, "I have heard that there are new treatments for seasickness. Maybe you should see the doctor."

Mrs. Cooper was tired of watching her daughter suffer and nodded in the affirmative. "I will take her just as soon as she is able to go."

"When you are well enough, I should like to teach you how to play chess. It is a wonderful distraction and helps to pass the time," Clark said to Natalie.

"I should like that very much," she replied as the men turned to leave.

Mrs. Cooper closed the door and said, "First thing in the morning, after your tea and crackers, we will take you to the doctor."

"Thank you, Mama."

December 11, 1875
Day 10

Dr. Danneman was a man of professional business. Though genial, he was primarily interested in the welfare of his patients and therefore allowed himself little distraction.

When he learned that Natalie had suffered similarly on her crossing from New York to France on the very same ship, he wished that he had been made aware so that he could have helped.

"Miss Cooper, why is it that I am seeing you just now and not sooner?"

"Mother has been taking care of me, and we didn't want to bother you since it is only seasickness."

"Seasickness is a very serious matter, and it is my job to help with all kinds of illnesses. Promise me that if you should ever find yourself sick on this ship again that you will come to me immediately."

"I promise," she replied.

After a brief examination he turned to Mrs. Cooper and said, "Let's try this first. Seasickness is a problem with equilibrium. The ears are a part of what helps us with that. Her ears are quite impacted with wax, so I propose to clean them out and see if it helps. Maybe it is just a matter of her being able to regain the proper pressure in her ears.

After performing the simple procedure, they waited for signs of improvement. None came.

"Close your eyes, Natalie. Do you find any relief at all?"

She nodded. "A little."

"I am going to cover your ears as well and see if you find any additional comfort. Please wait until I ask if it is helping."

Dr. Danneman covered her ears and waited a full five minutes. Then he lifted one of the ear covers and asked, "How about now—anything?"

"Yes, better still."

"Some doctors believe that it is your brain getting confused that causes the seasickness. I am beginning to come to their way of thinking. This is what I propose to do: I want to put patches over your eyes to supply as much darkness as possible and then wrap your ears to take away all sound for a while. Are you willing to try it?"

Natalie whispered a timid "yes."

"Mrs. Cooper, your daughter will stay here in the infirmary for a few hours, and we will see if this helps. You are welcome to stay here as long as you like, or you can come and go as you wish."

Once she was all wrapped up, Natalie wanted to talk to someone, but she couldn't hear anything. At first her mother held her hand, but after a while she stopped, and Natalie wondered why. Maybe Dr. Danneman wanted as little external stimulation as possible, so she tried to relax.

It seemed to be several tedious hours before she found herself being unwrapped. She opened her eyes and saw two anxious faces looking over her. Dr. Danneman spoke first. "Your mother stayed at your side, and she observed a calmness come over you."

"It was the first time during the voyage that you looked well," added Mrs. Cooper. "How do you feel?"

Natalie could sense hope in her mother's voice. "I do feel a bit better, Mama."

The doctor continued, "I do not know how long—or even if—it will last. Let's have you stay here, maybe through the night. Your mother can read to you to pass the time. I don't want you up until I am sure you are improved."

After opening a small drawer, Dr. Danneman brought out a small reddish book. "This is a book by Charles Dickens called *A Christmas Carol*. Ever heard of it?"

Natalie had not.

"I just finished it, and it was most satisfactory. I would be happy to hear it again."

The next few hours rolled pleasantly by as Mrs. Cooper's voice transported Natalie to London and into Ebenezer Scrooge's life.

It was a lovely book, and Natalie approved of the change in Mr. Scrooge. She wished that she could keep Christmas always. For a long time she pondered how she could do this. Maybe every morning she could write, "If today were Christmas, I would . . ." and then figure it out from there? *That would not be necessary,* she decided. *All I need to do is follow Mother's example of giving service to keep Christmas always.*

December 12, 1875
Day 11

Captain Norbert Duckwitz had been in command of the S. S. *Frisia* for only a few years, having taken over from Captain Meier. The Hamburg-American Line was rightly proud of their captain, and he in turn was proud of their ship. There were many who persisted that Captain Duckwitz was one of the best—a patriarch of the line with thirty-eight years of service. If he were to wear all the medals bestowed upon him, his uniform would look like a case in a jeweler's shop. A hale and jovial man, Captain Duckwitz was approachable and popular with his ocean travelers as well as with his crew.

On this morning, as he walked the deck enjoying the sunrise, he was met by Dr. Danneman.

"Captain, may I speak to you for a moment?"

"Yes, Doctor, certainly. What can I do for you?"

"Captain, I have a young lady in my infirmary whom I think you should meet."

"And why should this young lady interest me?"

"It's how she carries herself, Captain. She bears all her unhappiness without so much as a murmur. The girl has been terribly sick and still she keeps herself happy, especially considering her miserable situation. She reminds me much of your daughter Nessa when she was on board. They seem very much alike. I just thought you might like to meet her."

"Thank you, Doctor. I will make an effort to come by when I have a moment, but I can't say when."

"Yes, Captain. I understand. Thank you."

❋ ❋ ❋

Having spent the night in the infirmary, Natalie awoke and carefully lifted her head to see if she was really feeling better. Then she tried sitting up. She was still very weak, but her head—and stomach—were behaving properly for the moment. Mrs. Cooper, sensing Natalie's movements, aroused from her sleep and came to her. They were just beginning to discuss Natalie's new hope when the captain walked in with Dr. Danneman.

After introductions Captain Duckwitz said, "I remember seeing you board the ship some weeks ago. You were wearing a very pretty red bonnet, were you not?"

Natalie nodded. She was pleased that the captain had remembered her.

"How very happy I am to make your acquaintance. I only wish, however, that it was under better circumstances. Is our good doctor giving you his best care?"

Again Natalie nodded.

"Well, Miss Cooper, I want you to know that disagreeable weather in the Atlantic Ocean is something you may always count on. It tries the temperament of those who are saints on shore. The doctor tells me that you have the best disposition of any patient he has ever had, especially suffering as much as you have. Quite remarkable."

Natalie, not wanting to disappoint the captain by telling him what she thought of her disposition, simply said, "Thank you. I try."

"If the good doctor here should manage to make you well before tomorrow evening, I would like you and your mother to be my guests at the captain's table. It is a tradition on board. I host some of the passengers who might become important to our company, if you know what I mean."

Natalie replied, "I think I know what you mean," when really she didn't. She would ask her mother later.

"We will assume that you will be well enough to attend, and I will make sure that you have a proper place reserved. Until tomorrow, then." Tipping his cap to Natalie and her mother, he turned to leave.

"Thank you. You were right," he told Dr. Danneman as he passed through the door.

December 13, 1875
Day 12

As it turned out, Natalie was beginning to feel back to her old self (even though she was a very young self). For the first time in days everything smelled good and inviting to her. She and Mrs. Cooper were indeed seated in a "proper place," right between the captain and the doctor, just in case he was needed. Looking around Natalie saw a few of the people she had met on board. There were Mr. and Mrs. Hamblin as well as Mr. Miles and Clark. Whenever Natalie made eye contact with any of the guests she had met, they seemed wholly pleased the she was back on her feet, and they made little winks and nods in such ways as not to break the decorum of the sumptuous dinner. Natalie spent time remembering the goodness of all the people who had tried so hard to help her get well. She never wanted to be seasick again—ever.

Near the end of dinner Dr. Danneman said, "I think you are going to make it!"

Natalie said, "Yes, thank you. I think so as well."

Removing something from his dinner jacket he produced a little wrapped present and placed it quietly on her lap. "I think you know what it is. You don't need to open it here."

Natalie indeed knew. It was his copy of *A Christmas Carol*. Her wide eyes and big smile and rosy cheeks were all the thanks that Dr. Danneman could ask for.

Natalie and Mrs. Cooper left the captain's dinner having had the best evening of their voyage. On the way back to their stateroom to begin preparing to leave the ship, Natalie discovered that she was happy for the first time in weeks. As she walked she took out the book and unwrapped it, on the inside cover she found an inscription:

To Miss Natalie Cooper.

I could see that you love the Carol *as much as I do. I would like you to take care of this good book for me and share it with others. May you always find Christmas in your heart.*

With kindest regards, Dr. Brian Danneman

Embracing the book, she said, "I am going to try to keep Christmas in my heart always, just like Mr. Scrooge."

Natalie's thoughts were interrupted by a man standing next to her calling out, "Look there!" He pointed to a dark silhouette on the horizon. "Fire Island! We're almost home."

December 14, 1875
Her Change Complete

It was on the train ride home that Natalie's change was complete. She was grateful for all the people who had tried to help her, even though none of them had known her personally. Everyone had been ever so kind.

That day, though it was not yet Christmas, was the day that she kept Christmas. She *kept* it. She took its meanings into her heart and never let them go. She had learned— learned that love is the strongest force in the world. Every fiber of her being was changed to the point that she became her own person, independent of what anyone else thought of her. Natalie forgot herself and was now to find herself in others. She remembered a line from the Sophocles play *Ajax* that she had seen her mother reading that seemed appropriate: "Not for my sake but for thine." Even though it was a Greek tragedy, the line could point to the Lord. "Not for me, Lord, but for thee I will keep Christmas and always remember you." It was a commitment that she intended to keep.

December 16, 1875
Home

Mrs. Cooper was the first person into Mr. Cooper's arms, whereupon he planted an uninhibited kiss that assured her she had been missed. Natalie waited her turn, not wanting to spoil the moment. She rarely observed affection between her parents, and when she did, she liked it. It was her turn next, and she found herself lifted off the floor in the midst of a bear hug.

"I am very happy to have you both back. It's been like a morgue around here." Realizing his indiscretion, he immediately found his wife's eyes to see if he had wounded her.

Mrs. Cooper turned to her husband and said, "I am doing well, Nathan." She paused and then continued, "We both are."

Relieved, Mr. Cooper exclaimed, "I was going mad with you two gone. You can't imagine how happy I am to have you both home."

"Yes we can, Papa, because we are just as happy to be home," said Natalie.

"You mean I was missed?" he teased.

"Immensely," whispered Mrs. Cooper. "I have a surprise to tell you, but that will have wait."

Mr. Cooper's heart melted, and he wondered what the surprise could be.

July 23, 1876 (Natalie Is 11)
The Surprise

Christelle Elizabeth Cooper was welcomed to the Cooper household on July 23, 1876. She was a surprise in only one way: she was a blond-haired baby in a family of brunettes. She was a joy to behold.

Her birth distracted the family from the past and allowed them to focus on the future. Mrs. Cooper had come to terms with the death of Benjamin and became absorbed in the care of Christelle.

Natalie loved having the opportunity to take care of a baby, and Mrs. Cooper was grateful for the help. She enjoyed teaching Natalie how to do things the way her mother had done them and the way her mother's mother had done them.

August 8, 1876
Collin Bradley

The first time Collin saw her, she was doing what he liked best in the whole world: exploring. Her back was to him and she was looking intently at something on the bank of the Black River. Whatever it was, she appeared to be apprehensive about touching it. Looking around she found a dead stick and used it to lift up the curiosity. When he saw what was clinging to the stick, he let out a whistle of exclamation! The girl turned, and seeing Collin she asked, "Do you know what it is?"

Collin ran up to get a closer look. "I don't. It must be some kind of beetle bug." They were looking at a creature that was the length of a finger, with long, fierce pinchers.

"Do you think it bites?" she asked.

"I suspect it does," he said.

"I don't want to find out."

"I might give it a try," he said bravely.

She met the boy's eyes. "Might poison you!" she said concerned.

"Might just at that. Now I'm a thinkin' I won't." With that Collin found another stick to be the bait. When he teased the fearsome creature, it snapped its pinchers closed with lighting speed. Startled, both of them dropped their sticks, giggled with tense relief, and proceeded to reproduce the experiment. This time, however, the beetle had no intention of letting go of Collin's stick.

"What should we do with it?" he asked.

"Let it go, I suppose. I'm going to find out what it is from my father."

"We could drown it, and then you could show it to your pa."

"No, I don't want to harm it. I'll just draw him a picture. I have it well in my mind," she said with confidence.

Remembering his manners, Collin extended a hand to Natalie. "Collin Bradley. I'm twelve. We just moved here from New York."

"Natalie Cooper, eleven. Born and being raised here. Pleased to meet you," she reciprocated.

"Pleased to meet ya back," he said.

With that they left the beetle to its own devices and went on exploring the river together. Natalie showed Collin all of her favorite trees and rocks and little secret spots.

Collin in turn told Natalie about his trip from New York and that his father, who worked for the railroad, had been transferred to Chester to take over for the former station master. The whole family was looking forward to life in a small town that would hopefully be less hectic.

At noon Natalie declared that she had to get back home since the sun was straight up. "I'm allowed to explore only on Saturday mornings."

"How about I meet you here next Saturday and we can find more things together?"

After that Collin met Natalie as often as he could, never feeling the need to tell anyone, though it was very improper for a young girl and a young boy to be out and unattended together. It was all very secret—and very innocent.

February 14, 1877 (Natalie Is 12)
Valentine's Day

Natalie loved Valentine's Day. It was the only other day of the year where you could tell someone how you felt about them and not have to worry about propriety. It was almost like Christmas but not quite as much work. When she got to school she was disappointed to find that Mrs. Messing was substituting for Mrs. Trubl.

"I am Mrs. Messing," she announced. "Mrs. Trubl woke up this morning to find herself suddenly ill. I was asked to substitute at the last moment, as your regular substitute, Mr. Kincannon, is out of town."

The normal groans and sounds of disappointment were absent from the classroom because Mrs. Messing's reputation was known to most of the older children who had encountered her more often than not by being scolded for some minor infraction at church. They made sure the younger children stayed quiet.

Natalie's excitement for Valentine's Day quickly faded. She knew that Mrs. Messing didn't have a romantic bone in her body. Natalie had made valentines for everyone in class and had spent just a little more time on two of them—one for Mrs. Trubl and the other for Collin Bradley her new friend of six months.

Mrs. Messing continued, "When I learned that today was Valentine's Day I was most displeased, most displeased," she said, shaking her head.

Natalie stared straight at Mrs. Messing and whispered, "Here it comes."

"I have never celebrated it, and I believe that it is wasted time which would be better served learning something more important, like how to behave."

This time sounds of despair escaped from some of the children. Mrs. Messing raised a hand for silence and said, "However, Mrs. Trubl informed me about how important it was to her that you should have a proper Valentine's Day. Holding up a piece of paper she continued: "She wrote down specific instructions as to how we are to proceed. Since she is your teacher I will abide her instructions, though I wish that I didn't have to."

Natalie's relief was tempered by the realization that no matter what Mrs. Trubl wrote, Mrs. Messing would be sure to make it far less fun than if Mrs. Trubl were there.

"Number one tells me that everyone here is supposed to have brought a valentine for each member of the class. Everyone who has done so raise your hand." Mrs. Messing looked around and saw that Collin Bradley had not raised his hand. When Natalie saw this, she about choked, and a little tight knot formed in the pit of her stomach.

"You, young man, what is your name and why did you fail to bring valentines for the class?"

Collin stood up from his desk to address Mrs. Messing. "Collin Bradley, ma'am. I got them all made up and left them at the train station."

"Why the train station?"

"My father is station master, ma'am, and I was helping clean windows before school. He came out while I was washing them, with his watch in his hand, and said, 'Hurry along or you'll be late.' I did what he asked, and I left the valentines in his office."

"That is most unfortunate for you, Mr. Bradley, since you will not be allowed to participate in the day's activities," Mrs. Messing declared.

Mrs. Trubl had arranged her class in order of age, with the younger children up front and the oldest in the back. Collin was older, so he sat further back than Natalie did. Natalie turned around for a moment and met Collin's look of despair. She could see that he was on the verge of tears. The knot in her stomach grew even tighter because she knew that she would not be allowed to give Collin his valentine, and since Mrs. Trubl was absent, Natalie wouldn't be able to give her valentine either. This was just terrible.

Mrs. Messing read number two on the list: "We are to spend the morning with your normal studies, and after lunch you will be allowed to exchange your valentines. Number three, each student is to write their name on one of the boxes that Mrs. Trubl has collected for this purpose and place it on their desk. Four, at the proper time I am to let you place your valentines. She expects you older children to help the younger children who are still learning to read."

Natalie kept trying to think of a way that she could get herself excused, so that she could go to the train station and retrieve Collin's valentines. Everything she thought of involved some sort of lie, and Natalie just couldn't bring herself to do it. She decided that she would not be stopped. She would leave Mrs. Trubl's valentine on her desk and would give Collin his valentine after school.

Before lunch there was a knock on the school door. Mrs. Messing asked Brad Fullmer to go see who it was. When he came back he was being followed by Collin's father. Mr. Bradley walked up to Mrs. Messing and said, "I have brought Collin his lunch. May I give it to him?"

"Yes, Mr. Bradley, you may. We don't want your son to go without! Collin Bradley, please come here and get your lunch from your father," requested Mrs. Messing.

Natalie noticed that Collin could hardly contain a grin, as he walked back to his seat, lunch in hand. She almost never felt that way about food, but as Collin passed her he opened his sack, reached in, and produced his valentines for her to see, and then quickly put them back. Natalie felt very happy for him, and now she was going to be able to leave his valentine in his box. He would know it was from her.

At the appointed time for the exchange, Collin stood up with everyone else. Mrs. Messing said, "Mr. Bradley, you were told that you could not participate. Have your valentines magically appeared?"

"In a way, ma'am, yes. They were in with my lunch," he said, producing them for her to see.

"That is very fortunate for you, Mr. Bradley. You may proceed."

After the exchange, Natalie desired to see what her valentine from Collin looked like. He had made her a folded card consisting of white hearts. On the inside he had written, "To Miss Natalie Cooper. I have felt very welcome since coming to Chester and it has everything to do with you. I am in your debt and will always try to be your valentine." Natalie felt herself redden. She was touched and a little taken aback that he had said "always." She liked him too, but she had never encouraged him, not as far as she could see. Her valentine to him was not nearly so forward. All she had said was that she was happy to have him as her best boy friend. Natalie about choked when she realized what she had written. She had meant *boy* friend as opposed to *girl* friend, but it could be interpreted as boyfriend! That had to be made right directly.

She went over to Collin demanding to see the valentine she gave him. Natalie opened the valentine and underlined the word *boy* several times so that there would be no doubt about her intentions.

The exchange made enough commotion that it got the attention of Mrs. Messing, who came over to them demanding to see the valentine. As Natalie handed it to her she wanted to shrink into the floor. She was sure that Mrs. Messing was going to read it out loud to the class. Instead, Mrs. Messing handed the valentine to Collin and said to Natalie. "Very astute correction. Please take your seat."

Natalie could hardly believe her ears. Mrs. Messing had saved her. How terrible could she be?

June 2, 1878 (Natalie Is 13)
Trouble

Natalie sat watching the waterwheel at the mill go round and round. She wondered just how far it would have traveled had it been on a journey of its own instead of being a prisoner of work. If it had been free to travel anywhere it wanted, where would it go? She would have chosen the moon and guessed that the wheel would have made it to the moon by now and been well on its way home.

Suddenly she detected a little interruption in the wheel's rhythm. Had she really seen it? Staring intently, she watched for it to happen again, and after a while it did. Watching longer she discovered that it occurred at regular intervals. Fear rose inside of her. Everyone knew the waterwheel could never stop—ever! It wasn't so much that she really believed that the world would end if the wheel stopped, but there were others who believed that it would. Natalie had no intention of raising the alarm to anyone other than her father, and she ran to find him.

Nathan Cooper followed Natalie to the waterwheel and sat with her watching for what she had described.

"I see it," he said.

"What is it, Papa?"

"A cracked bearing, I suspect, or maybe the shaft is wearing out. Fortunately for us you noticed it early, so we have some time to prepare.

"Is it serious?"

"Very. Anytime there is a threat that could stop the wheel it's serious. The legend has been good to us, and I don't propose to find out what would happen if the wheel should stop beyond the traditional time for repairs."

"Has this problem happened before, Papa?"

"Not while we have owned the mill. We have had to do minor repairs and maintenance, but this problem is a new one."

"When will you fix it?"

"I don't know yet. Because of the legend, all repairs must take place during the full moons of summer. I will have to look and see when the next one is to occur, and then we will have to prepare very carefully. I'm going to need help—and from people who are capable and not too worried about the legend. This work has to be performed in a calm environment. There can be no mistakes. Let's go tell your mother and start making plans."

Mr. Cooper went to consult the *Farmer's Almanac*. He learned that the next full moons were to occur on June 26 and July 25. He would prepare for June, and if he missed that opportunity, he would have July.

It had been a good many years since the wheel had been replaced, so Mr. Cooper decided to replace it entirely, which should buy him twenty years or more before he had to do it again.

In the ensuing days and weeks the interruption became more than noticeable; it had turned into a lurch and with every revolution the wheel was becoming more unbalanced.

Everything in the Cooper household centered on preparing for the replacement of the waterwheel. Everyone was tense. Mr. Cooper always kept problems with the waterwheel as secret as he could. There was no need to alarm the town. He explained the seriousness of people's superstitions to Natalie, and he hoped she understood that under no circumstances was she to tell anyone about the problem.

Mr. Cooper used the barn to construct a new waterwheel as well as an A-frame and scaffolding that he would need to support the weight of the wheel. The scaffolding had to be designed in such a way that it would go up quickly and come down even faster.

The June full moon was missed because the new wheel was not ready. Mr. Cooper was taking great care in the new wheel's construction. He used the best oak he could find, and he was confident that this wheel was as strong as it could possibly be. "Who knows," he said to Natalie, "it might last thirty years."

By the middle of July the waterwheel was in serious jeopardy of failing. Watching it turn was painful because they could see the stress on the old timbers. There was an audible screeching every time it made one of its eternal revolutions. Every day Mrs. Cooper prayed at family dinner for the wheel to keep turning as it always had.

As the next full moon approached, everything was ready.

On the appointed night Natalie walked under her stars, the tender light of the rising full moon accompanying her to the mill. She was excited to be helping her father with this important job. Her task was to attend to the lanterns and provide light wherever needed. Her mother usually performed this task, but it fell to Natalie this night because Mrs. Cooper needed to care for Christelle, who was only two.

After the full moon had risen, Mr. Cooper stopped the waterwheel. It was a strained moment for the five workmen. They waited until Mr. Cooper broke the tension. "We're still here," he remarked, "so I guess we had better just get the job done."

Mr. Cooper and the other men proceeded to replace the wheel. In the first hours the scaffolding was set up and the A-frame placed up over the old wheel.

The large A-frame was a simple design that would work well with block and tackle. Once everything was in place, the old wheel was lifted so that the pins could be pulled out and the shaft slid out. It was during this part of the operation that they heard a loud pop. Work stopped immediately. An inspection of the structure did not show the source of the sound. A discussion ensued. No one could agree on exactly what they had heard, so they continued. The old wheel was lowered and rolled out of position, and the new one was rolled up the raceway.

Being made of new wood and of better construction, the new wheel was heavier than the old one. While the A-frame was under the full load of the new wheel, one of its legs snapped about two feet from the bottom. This set the wheel crashing to the bed of the raceway, and the men scrambled to hold it there.

Examining the break, they discovered that one of legs of the A-frame had been weak in the center, and they now knew the source of the "pop." Mr. Cooper realized in a fury that he had forgotten to sound the wood by striking it with a mallet to hear if it would ring true. That simple test would have saved him this misery. With the A-frame out of commission the work stopped and the men realized that they were not going to get the task completed before sunup.

"Any ideas on how to keep the world from ending?" asked Mr. Cooper, scanning the distressed faces turned toward him.

Natalie felt like she had been punched in the stomach. She stood up from where she had been sitting on an old millstone. It was no longer useful for grinding and was too big to easily discard. She wanted a better look at the break while the men were trying to figure out what to do. The situation looked hopeless to her. Returning back to the millstone seat, she sat down, but this time she missed her mark and found the center of the stone with her bottom. That made her take notice of the hole in it. A thought occurred to her. Standing up, she looked the stone over and called, "Papa, what about this?"

Mr. Cooper came over. "What are you thinking, Natalie?"

"Papa, this stone—it looks to be about the same thickness as the piece of wood that broke off. If you were to use it as a prop and place the leg in the hole, would that work?"

Mr. Cooper caught the vision of her idea immediately and called the men over. Everyone agreed that it should work, and they proceeded with new hope and energy.

It was all the six of them could do to get the old millstone moved and the A-frame lifted. Once it was in place, the millstone was just a little thicker than it needed to be; however they elected to give it a try.

As the new wheel was lifted with block and tackle suspended from the A-frame, the increased weight caused the broken leg of the A-frame to settle tight into the hole of the old millstone, balancing the new waterwheel. Everything was now in alignment, as it should have been in the first place. The shaft for the new wheel was slid through and new pins were set. Thankfully the scaffolding came down easily and the A-frame was disassembled with the exception of the broken leg that was now firmly stuck in the old millstone. Mr. Cooper decide to just let it stay there as a little monument to Natalie's creative thinking.

Just before the full moon set behind the trees, the new waterwheel was turning. Mr. Cooper walked over to Natalie and tousled her hair like she had seen him do to Benjamin. Smiling at her in the light of dawn, he said, "How does it feel to know that you saved the world?"

"Pretty nice if I really did."

"You certainly saved the world as far as I'm concerned!"

Natalie felt wonderful and skipped all the way back to the house, eager to tell her mother about the excitement.

Winter 1880
Mr. Hope

Fifteen-year-old Natalie met Mr. Hope when he stumbled into her while she was coming out of Mrs. Adams's General Store. He practically knocked her over, and in attempting to miss her he stumbled and fell to the ground. She tried to help him up, and only together could they manage to do it. Natalie found herself looking into a pugnacious wind-burned face that had seen many unpleasant years. This incident reminded her of the first time she had seen Mrs. Messing.

When she asked the man where he lived, his face became very sorrowful. A tear trickled down his cheek and he replied, "Wherever I happen to be standing at the moment." Her suspicion that the speaker had been drinking was confirmed by a blast of noxious breath.

Natalie was most dissatisfied. She sat him down on the bench outside the store and said, "Wait right here."

He looked at her with glazed eyes, sloppily nodded, and said, "Yes, ma'am."

Natalie was surprised that she had never seen the man before. Going back into the store she asked Mrs. Adams about him. "Mrs. Adams, could you please tell me about the old man I left outside?"

"That's Mr. Hope, pickled to the gills as always. No one knows his first name, and even he can't remember it. He's always telling people that he is the unluckiest man that ever walked the earth. For whatever reason, the citizens of Chester have taken pity on him and have helped him time and time again, and time and time again he has disappointed them.

"Maybe it's his name that has led people to have pity on him or maybe it's his stories about having served in the Civil War and losing near his whole family. Heaven knows I really don't know why. He's a likable old cuss when he's sober. And when he's not, he disgorges his offenses of smell and dirt and life upon whomever he meets on the street."

Natalie, looking herself over, said, "I seem to have acquired some of his offenses," while trying in vain to brush herself off. "I can't recall ever seeing him."

"Well, he's up all hours of the night drinking while you are at home sleeping, where you should be, and Mr. Hope almost always sleeps during the day. Still, people continue to help him."

"I plan to as well. Thank you, Mrs. Adams."

Natalie took charge of things in her competent way. She helped Mr. Hope to her home and got him cleaned up. She decided that Mr. Hope was going to be her special cause and that she was going to get him well. A few days later she found a place for him to stay. It was on the McDonald property, which lay between the Cooper Mill and Chester. They had a small building that was originally built to be a chicken coop. When the McDonalds built the coop and saw their house burn down, they furnished the coop to make it livable for themselves. After they got their new home built, they no longer wanted to use it for chickens and left it as it was when they had lived in it. They had no problem letting Mr. Hope stay until they might need it.

Natalie checked on him as often as time would allow, and she convinced her father to let him help at the mill. When Mr. Hope did show up for work, he was most helpful. The problem was that he missed more days than he worked, and Mr. Cooper told Natalie that Mr. Hope was hurting the mill's business by not getting his allotted work done. After Mr. Hope missed three days in a row, Mr. Cooper had to let him go. Natalie was unhappy with her father at first, but she soon came to understand his reasons.

❊ ❊ ❊

A few weeks later Natalie saw another need of Mr. Hope's. His gloves—or what was left of them—were nearly useless. She determined to rectify the situation.

Looking at the results she held in her hands, her critical eye would not let her like them, but they would have to do. The gloves would serve their purpose. While not handsome, they would keep Mr. Hope's hands warm. He needed the gloves, and Natalie was determined that he would get them as soon as possible.

"Papa?" called Natalie, "Would you come and try these on for me?"

Mr. Cooper entered the kitchen to see his daughter holding a pair of tan, calfskin-leather gloves.

"For Mr. Hope," she said, holding them out to him.

Her father obligingly pulled them on. They were just a little too tight for him, which exposed a few flaws. "Look here," he said, "I can see my fingers here and here and here and here," pointing to several places in the seams where the stitching was not tight enough.

"Thanks, Papa. I was afraid of that. My fingers have become sore from rushing to get the gloves done, so I haven't had my normal strength for tight stitches. Could you help me?"

"Yes. What do you need?"

"Take them off and help me to get them closed up tight. I will show you what to do." Whereupon Natalie and Mr. Cooper finished Natalie's gift together. This time the results were more to her satisfaction.

"Thank you, Papa," she said, giving him a quick peck on the cheek. "I'm off to take these to Mr. Hope. I'll be back soon."

"Very good," he said, adding, "I'm sure they will work very nicely, considering that his hands are smaller than mine."

Natalie set off on her journey. The walk to the little coop house took only a few minutes. Natalie was sure Mr. Hope would still be home, for he was a late sleeper, usually brought on as a result of his drinking. After reaching the front door she began to knock—and knock and knock. It was like trying to wake the dead. Her knuckles became so sore from knocking that she put on Mr. Hope's gloves to continue the resurrection attempt. Just as she was about to give up, she heard a noise and the door opened.

"Oh, Miss Cooper! Do come in, do come in. Were you waiting long?"

"Not very," she said aloud, adding silently to herself, *in terms relative to eternity.*

"Oh good, oh good. Sometimes I learns later that I have missed company coming, on account of my condition. I would have been sorely disappointed had I missed you."

"I brought you these," she told him, holding up her hands to show him the gloves.

"I put them on so I could continue knocking." She reddened at being caught in her little white lie, but she chose not to respond further. Instead she took off the gloves and proceeded to help him put them on.

"Oh! I did keep you waiting. I am sorry. He held up his hands and admired them. My! They sure do fit nice. Warm too. I can already tell. I might even wear 'em to bed. Gets cold some nights when I forgets to stoke the stove on account of my condition."

Natalie worried that his "condition" would also cause him to forget to wear the gloves.

"Mr. Hope, I want you to take good care of these. We don't need you to get frostbitten hands. It would be most inconvenient."

"For me too, Miss Cooper."

"Yes, that's what I meant. You need your hands, and I'm sure those old gloves of yours provide no comfort."

"Yes, ma'am. They gave up their comfort a number of winters ago."

"That long?" exclaimed Natalie, distressed that no one had seen fit to replace them.

"No matter. I have these now, and I sure do appreciate them. I'm likely not to take them off all day, considering how nice they feel."

"That wouldn't be practical, and besides, if you wear them too much, you won't have them for when you really need them, now would you?" she scolded kindly.

"No, I suppose you're right. I promise I will make them last."

"Now, is there anything else I can help you with before I have to go?"

"Could you help me with my laces?" he said with a grin, holding up the gloves on his hands. "I'm not ready to take them off yet, and besides, my rheumatism is making it difficult for my hands to work just now."

Looking down at his shoes, she saw that he had not taken the time to lace them up.

"Mr. Hope, what are we going to do with you?" she gently chided as she knelt down and tied his shoes.

Natalie stood up and put her hands on her hips. "I think we're going to have to put some brains into that head of yours," she added teasingly.

"Well, if you do, when I gets used to using my brains, I shall know everything indeed. That reminds me, my old school teacher Mr. Horner said I was built kinda backwards because my nose ran and my feet smelled. I never forgot it."

Natalie chuckled but said nothing.

Mr. Hope took Natalie's hands in his. "I'm very much obliged to you, Miss Cooper. Thank you."

Natalie gave his hands a squeeze and started for home, happy with Mr. Hope's happiness.

❉ ❉ ❉

When March arrived the town council, led by Mrs. Messing, decided that they were no longer going to allow Mr. Hope to sleep off his drunken stupors at the jail. The law required that breakfast be provided to anyone who stayed the night, and he had taken the town's generosity to extremes. He was told that when he got drunk he would have to make it home on his own. Two weeks later Mr. Hope was found frozen, facedown in the snow after a night of drinking—wearing the gloves that Natalie had given him. Since he died so soon after being informed of the council's decision, their last act of kindness toward him was to see that he had a proper marker at the cemetery to ease their feelings of guilt.

Natalie was very distraught over losing Mr. Hope. She had come to love the old man. She learned that if people are going to have any chance at all to make it in life, they need the help of others, just like she had had aboard the S. S. *Frisia* a few years back. Mr. Hope had been a human being—alive, with a soul and feelings like everyone else. She recommitted to helping as many people as she could, and, unbeknownst to her, she continued to grow into one of the favorite citizens of Chester.

April 1880 (Natalie Is 15)
Thoughts

Spring was upon the world. Natalie found herself sitting outside in the fresh air and sunshine daydreaming. Ever since she had first seen Collin on the bank of the Black River she had been attracted to him. As they grew older she was very careful to keep him at a proper distance in case he turned out to be different than she supposed him to be. Deep inside she knew that no other boy was going to do—even though Collin was a full three inches shorter than she was.

He was a good-looking fellow. He had a frankness and maturity that earned him respect among the other young men, and his deferential chivalry appealed to the girls. This combination of characteristics afforded him many friends.

What was more, Collin had an infectious smile and was one of the few people who had the ability to make her laugh. She felt really alive around him and imagined that together they could make the world anything they wanted to make it. Everything she saw and learned about Collin was a new source of joy. She was charmed and interested and considered him to be a choice and worthy young man.

Over the years there were times when Natalie had caught Collin looking at her, and when their eyes met, his were always the first to flee. It was as if he was looking into her soul, and it sent fiery flushes all the way down to her toes.

The thought that he was interested in her made her happy. She hoped the attraction would last until the proper time, so she was very careful not to let him know how she really felt about him.

There was only one thing that Natalie didn't like about Collin: his last name. She had tried it out a number of times and just couldn't get used to the name Natalie Bradley. However she had no problem with Mrs. Collin Bradley. It was a small price to pay should things work out the way that she hoped.

❄ ❄ ❄

At times Collin felt shy and tongue-tied around Natalie, though he worked hard not to show it. He was sure he didn't have a chance for a future with her, especially since she was a full three inches taller than he was. They had played together as children and had spent many a day lost in their favorite haunts, yet he was sure that she felt just enough sympathy for him that she let him stay around. He didn't mind, because it meant that he got to be close to her.

He resolved to remain hopeful that over time she might change her mind about him. He would continue to be himself and show his affection for her in the best ways he could. For him, love was something sacred that called for quiet voices and sunsets. He would take his time.

July 23, 1880 (Natalie Is 15, Christelle Is 4)
Petticoat Tails

When Natalie answered the door she found Collin Bradley standing there, looking hopeful.

"Yes, Mr. Bradley, what can I do for you?"

"I was wondering if you might like to go fishing."

"Yes, very much, but I can't. Today is Christelle's birthday, and we are getting ready to make petticoat tails. Would you like to postpone your fishing to stay and help us make them?"

"Petticoat tails, Miss Cooper? Do you think I should help you make such a thing? It sounds just a little scandalous."

"You're telling me that you have never made petticoat tails?"

Shaking his head, he asked, "Should I have?"

Nodding her head, she took him by the arm and declared, "It's time to expand your education, Mr. Bradley." Whereupon she led him to the kitchen.

"Mama, Mr. Bradley has never heard of petticoat tails, so I invited him to help us."

"I suppose he could be of some use. Are you useful, Mr. Bradley?"

"I try to be, Mrs. Cooper."

"We shall hope that you are!"

Collin sincerely hoped that petticoat tails were not what the name implied. For if they were, he would find it hard to forgive Natalie for this kind of expanded education.

"Have a seat, Mr. Bradley, while we get things ready," said Mrs. Cooper.

The big mixing bowl was Collin's first clue that the name petticoat tails gave no clue as to what they were, but it relieved his fear of embarrassment. The butter, flour, and sugar led him to understand that he was going to get a baking lesson.

"Petticoat tails are shortbread cookies," explained Natalie. "They are a Cooper favorite."

"The name comes from *petits gastelles,* which means little cakes, in French," added Mrs. Cooper. "My mother taught me how to make them, and I taught Natalie, and now we are going to teach Christelle and now you."

"Natalie, would you please find your sister? I told her that we were going to make a surprise for her birthday and that she could help."

Natalie came into the kitchen with a bouncing Christelle in tow asking, "What? What? What do I get to do, Mama?"

"You get to add the flour."

Christelle considered this. "I be back," she responded and then skipped out of the kitchen.

When she returned, Mrs. Cooper was showing Collin the recipe, which was simple enough—one part sugar, two parts butter, and three parts flour. Christelle was only noticed after she announced, "I added the flower." She spoke in a satisfied voice while peering into the mixing bowl.

Her mother, Natalie, and Collin followed her gaze and saw that a single blue flower had been placed in the bowl.

"Very good, Christelle," said Mrs. Cooper, smiling, "but we need to add a different kind of flour." She removed the flower and handed it to Collin, saying, "Take care of this, please."

Collin didn't know what kind of care she meant. First he considered putting it in Natalie's hair, but he didn't want to appear too forward. He decided to play it safe and placed the flower in the lapel of his vest. Collin's solution made the ladies smile.

"Now, Mr. Bradley, would you please help Christelle put the flour in the mixing bowl while I add a little molasses to the sugar?"

Collin handed Christelle the cups of flour to dump. Christelle sprang forward toward the mixing bowl. Natalie, seeing disaster looming, grabbed the mixing bowl and intercepted the flour that was being dumped out.

"Mr. Bradley, if you hand a four-year-old a cup of flour, you hand it to them over the bowl. That way you won't have a mess or possibly end up wearing the flour yourself."

"Thank you for saving me. I would rather not get floured today, since I had my weekly dose of flour only yesterday while baking bread with my mother."

"Baking bread, Mr. Bradley? Are you planning on becoming a baker or maybe a domestic?"

"I am not really sure, Miss Cooper. It depends on how useful that would be. We will just have to wait and see."

Mrs. Cooper turned to Natalie, "Daughter, would you please go and find your father? He has taken the raisins for elevenses, and I forgot that I was going to need some for the shortbread. Please bring back whatever is left."

"Yes, Mama," replied Natalie obediently as she walked to the back door of the kitchen. Finding that it was windy, Natalie took a moment to tie back her long wavy hair. This caught Christelle's attention.

"Sis has pretty hair," she said.

"She has pretty everywhere," whispered Collin to the little girl sitting on his lap. But he hadn't been quiet enough, and Mrs. Cooper had overheard.

As Natalie left she caught her mother's eyes and was puzzled to see them full of mischief. Mrs. Cooper had a little half smile that Natalie had come to know. It meant she was going to have some fun at someone's expense—this time Collin's. Natalie walked with hesitation, wondering what was going to happen. Then she hiked up her skirts, deciding to hurry.

The banging of the mill's big door alerted Mr. Cooper to Natalie's presence.

"Papa, do you have any raisins left?" she asked breathlessly.

"Why the hurry?"

"Mama's going to tease Collin. I may need to save him."

"Did she have that look in her eyes?"

"Yes!"

"Oh my. He hasn't got a chance. Raisins are on the bench. Better run along."

With that Natalie grabbed the little sack and ran for the house.

As she approached the kitchen a little winded, she paused when she heard her mother say, "Are you in love with my daughter, Mr. Bradley?"

"Pardon!?" exclaimed Collin, completely caught off guard.

"Are you in love with my daughter?"

"I don't understand your question, Mrs. Cooper."

"It is quite simple enough, Mr. Bradley. You have placed a bachelor button in your lapel, and tradition has it that only a young man in love wears the bachelor button flower. You placed it there while here in my home, so I can only assume that it must mean it is my daughter Natalie who you are in love with, since Christelle is much too young."

Natalie couldn't help it: a big smile was having its way with her face as she entered the kitchen. She looked at her mother, amused by what was taking place—but even more so by what Collin was going to say.

Collin's embarrassment swelled to a torrent. "I . . . I . . . I . . ." he stammered.

Mrs. Cooper seemed to wait for an interminable time before she continued. "We shall know soon enough, Mr. Bradley. The legend states that if the flower fades quickly, your love is not real."

Collin didn't know where to look or what to say. With his mind swimming for lack of an answer, he could only look from Natalie's face to her mother's and then back again. This went on for some moments before he found relief by staring straight down at the floor.

"Mother, that was a mean thing to do," reproved Natalie gently. Mrs. Cooper only chuckled and mixed the raisins into the remaining dough. While the tension dissipated Collin secretly hoped that the flower would never wither.

Their noses told them that the first batch of petticoat tails was done. Mrs. Cooper cut them into triangles and handed the first one to Christelle. She ate it quickly and asked for more. Mrs. Cooper gave her two more. Christelle devoured them, and when she reached for still more her mother warned, "Christelle, don't eat too many; they may give you a tummy ache!"

"Momma, they are so good. I want a tummy ache!"

"I think not," declared Mrs. Cooper, "but thank you for the nice compliment."

Christelle's look of disappointment yielded her one more cookie. She immediately smiled and ran out to play.

Natalie approached Collin as he was finishing his second helping.

"It's their shape that makes them petticoat tails," she informed him.

"I am very happy to make their acquaintance, especially with my teeth," he said as he chomped his last bite. "It is a relief to know what they are now, rather than what I thought they were. I quite heartily approve, Miss Cooper. Thank you for letting me help you. I will never forget today."

"With the position that mama put you in, I should think you wouldn't. Here, let me take care of that flower for you." Collin intercepted Natalie's hand, gently pulling it away from the flower.

Meeting Natalie's eyes he said, "please, I would very much like to keep it."

Natalie didn't know what to say, and she felt a blush come to her cheeks.

"I will see you later, and maybe we can go fishing," continued Collin. "Please thank your mother for me and tell Christelle happy birthday one more time for me, will you?"

Natalie nodded in the affirmative as Collin took his leave.

March 9, 1881 (Natalie Is 16)
Kite Day

Kite day was Mrs. Trubl's way of getting the students outside after being cooped up for the winter. It always came sometime in March, depending on the weather. February had been particularly warm, to the point that the little blue saffron crocus flowers had started to bloom, but then it had turned wet and windy. It was the windy part that everyone had been waiting for with eager anticipation.

On kite day at Chester School, it was expected that everyone should have a kite to fly. It was a great deal of work to get things ready, and this year, if everything went well, there would be twenty-two kites in the air.

The plan for the day was always the same. Kite construction and decoration took place in the morning. The finished kites were left to dry near the wood stove through the noon hour while everyone had a picnic on the floor. After cleaning up from all the activity, everyone went outside in the afternoon to fly the kites.

This year Mrs. Trubl asked Collin, who had graduated the previous year, to come back and help with kite day. The reason was simple: he made the best kites, and just by looking at a kite in the progress of being built he could tell you how it was going to fly. His help ensured that more kites got into the air.

Collin had made many kites and knew the tricks of the trade: Tying the cross sticks together kept them from sliding. Bowing the kite just right helped it to catch the wind. The bridle had to be at the proper angle for a kite to lift easily in the wind. Adding a little longer tail always made the kites that were out of balance fly better. Most of the younger children had longer tails attached to their kites.

❄ ❄ ❄

Collin looked over Natalie's shoulder to see if she needed any help. Her kite interested him because he had never seen one like it. The kite was only about 8 inches long and paddle shaped like those new light bulbs. At that moment she was attaching broom straws for the sticks.

"Miss Cooper?"

"Yes, Mr. Bradley?"

"What are you making there?"

"A broomstraw kite! I saw the pattern for it in a craft book at home, so I decided to make one. I wanted to have the smallest kite in the whole world . . . well, at least here in Chester."

"I am sorry to inform you, Miss Cooper, but there are smaller kites."

"Can you prove it, Mr. Bradley? I would like to think I have the smallest kite in the world. That was what I wanted to do today."

To answer her question, Collin handed her a small box. "I brought you a little present for kite day," he told her. The box made a rattling sound when she shook it, and after opening it, she was puzzled because the item inside was most unimpressive.

"And what precisely am I supposed to do with a spool of thread?"

"It is to make sure that this does not escape," he replied, handing her another little box. "And please, do not shake this one. You might damage what's inside."

Natalie took great care in opening this box. What was inside surprised and delighted her. "How perfectly lovely—a baby kite. It is very cute!" she exclaimed, quite charmed by Collin's gesture.

"The smallest kite in the world, I should think, and I made it just for you. If you look carefully, you will see that you are part of it."

Natalie did indeed look carefully at the tiny creation. It had the classic kite shape and was at most two inches long. It was made from a small piece of tin foil, with blue thread for a tail. Upon closer examination she could see that it had little broom straws for the cross sticks.

"I can see that you have also thought to use broom straws," she remarked.

"Yes, it seemed only natural given its tiny size."

Natalie could see a tiny loop at the end of a single strand of thread. When she lifted it up, the kite appeared to be floating in the air. The bridle was made of hair!

"Hair, Mr. Bradley?"

"Your hair, Miss Cooper. I obtained them from your coat whenever I spied one. It took only a few. So you see, you are also part of the kite."

"Mr. Bradley, are you telling me that together we have made a baby kite?"

Reddening, Collin stuttered, "Well, yes, sort of—uh—I only meant . . ."

Saving Collin, she quickly added, "I will treasure it and keep it safe always."

"We can go fly it if you wish," he suggested.

"Oh no, Mr. Bradley. It is much too small to fly just now. We should wait until it grows up. Then we will let it fly. I will even let you watch it take its first flying steps." Natalie continued to explore the little creation with her eyes before asking, "What do you feed baby kites?"

"What?"

"What do you feed baby kites?"

"Uh . . . wind."

"Wind?"

"Yes, wind. The more you feed them wind, the larger they will grow."

"But it is much too young for wind just yet. I think that we should start with just a little puff of air or two, don't you? And once we get it weaned off little puffs of air, we should move on to breezes. Then when breezes are no longer enough, we shall feed it lots of wind. Does this meet with your approval, Mr. Bradley?"

"Yes, Miss Cooper, but I am telling you that we can fly it now."

"Are you telling me that I should risk my new baby kite before we have even become acquainted? Unless you can give me one very good reason why we should fly it, I am going to wait until it grows up some. We new mothers are very protective, you know!"

"Very well, Miss Cooper," said Collin, resigned to the fact that he was not going to win this little tête-à-tête.

Natalie continued, "Since you have given me such a lovely little treasure, I shall give you one of my own." Where upon she handed him her completed broomstraw kite. "For you, Mr. Bradley."

Collin was surprised to receive the kite.

"It is already big enough to handle breezes," she said with a twinkle in her eye.

"Maybe, Miss Cooper, but I intend to wait until it can fly with the baby."

"Like I said, you must provide me with a good reason."

For the rest of kite day Collin and Natalie spent their time helping the other children fly their kites. Collin wanted very much for Natalie to fly her miniature kite, and he was trying to come up with a reason why she should do it. Natalie as well wanted desperately to try out both kites, but she had teased herself into a corner, and now she was stuck. Collin was the only one who could let her out.

After all of the other children had gone home, Collin and Natalie helped Mrs. Trubl clean up the remains of the small disasters that had occurred during kite day. There were always broken kites, some beyond repair. The ones that found themselves in the trees were left to Mother Nature's devices for removal. Wind and rain did most of the work, and birds needing nesting materials took care of the rest.

The day was almost over when Collin came up with a good reason.

"Miss Cooper?"

"Yes?"

"I seem to recall that baby kites are just like baby ducks."

"Baby ducks? I don't see the connection."

"Baby ducks can swim right after they hatch, and baby kites can fly right after they are made."

"Knowing that would have saved me a lot of fuss and concern," she reproached.

"Shall we?" asked Collin.

Natalie, freed from her corner, was delighted at how well the world's smallest kite flew. She was able to get it up twenty feet before the weight of the thread held it back. Likewise, Collin was surprised to learn that the broomstraw kite flew very well, even with its paper tail.

They flew their kites together sitting side by side until the setting sun took the wind away for the evening. The beauty of the cloudy sunset was a perfect ending to kite day.

Sisters, portrait of Natalie and Christelle Cooper
painted by Alexei Alexeievich Harlamoff (1842–1925).

Part Two

The waterwheel, turning year after year, day after day, minute after minute had counted sixteen years, ten months, one week, and three days since Natalie was born in the year of our Lord 1864.

November 1881
The Cooper Grist Mill

"Papa!" called Natalie, "Papa, where are you?"

"Here, child. I'm over here stacking sacks. What is it?"

"Can we begin Christmas early this year?"

"What do you mean *this* year? You begin Christmas early every year!"

"I want to start making my presents much earlier. I want to do the Christmas tree and everything."

"Why?"

"Because I want to make Christmas last longer."

"And when do you want to start?"

"Now!"

"Now? But it's only the first of November. This family starts making Christmas in the middle of December after I get all the milling done. You know how busy we are!"

"If I help you with the mill, can we start now?"

"Let me think about it for a bit." Nathan Cooper, covered in flour dust, stood considering. His oldest daughter had always been drawn to Christmas. Her life centered around it, and how often Christmas had visited during the other eleven months of the year he couldn't even begin to count, but she made it so. It seemed that Christmas was always there, just under her skin, part of the fabric that she was made of. To say that she was a ray of sunshine was wholly inadequate. She *was* sunshine. She lit up everyone she met. Everyone loved her—everyone.

"Well Papa?"

"I guess so. I don't see why not, but the tree will have to wait until the usual time. We don't want it to dry out and become a fire danger to the house."

"I know, Papa. Green is safe; with brown it's not. I remember what you tell me." Natalie bounced up to her father and quickly kissed him, removing some of the flour dust from his cheek.

As she danced and twirled out of the room, he called to her, "Natalie, I might need to take you up on your offer to help, depending on how busy you keep me getting ready for Christmas."

She stopped, nodded in affirmation, and said, "I'm off to find my bonnet."

"Some of the town folk might lift an eyebrow to see her wearing it in November," Mr. Cooper said to himself as he turned back to his work.

Natalie paused and called out, "Papa, guess what? Christmas is on a Sunday this year." She sang as she skipped off, the melody of "Jingle Bells" ringing through the trees.

November 5, 1881
Errands

She certainly knows how to delight the eye, thought Collin. "Look at you, Miss Cooper. All dressed up and wearing that pretty red bonnet. Are we not just a little early this year?" he teased.

"Yes, we are, Mr. Bradley. I want this to be the best Christmas ever."

"You say that every year, and yet you somehow manage to make it come true. And where are we headed?"

"*I* am headed for Mrs. Adams's store."

"May I accompany you and keep you safe from any highwaymen that might happen by?"

"I think I can manage, thank you."

"Are you sure?"

"Yes, Mr. Bradley. Thank you. I think highwaymen are rather scarce here in town, and if I remember correctly, shouldn't you be helping your father over at the depot at this hour?"

"Yes, you are right. But he sent me to the General Store for a few things. Here's my list," replied Collin, pulling a paper from his pocket. "So you'll just have to put up with me anyway, Miss Cooper."

"Very well, but only for as long as we are in the store," she said, giving him a vigorous push on the shoulder then running for the store.

Collin, caught off guard, ran after her. Just before she reached the store he had barely enough time to return the push, though not with quite as much force.

Mrs. Adams's General Store was the lifeblood of Chester. Mrs. Adams was a dealer in dry goods and groceries, the postmaster, and an agent for the newspaper in Bedminster, a few miles away. Her establishment also provided a gathering place for the residents of Chester where they could get not only the latest household goods but also the latest news and local gossip.

Upon entering the store one encountered a long and slender room with beautifully polished floors. The left side was lined with shelves of groceries and a case for candy. Next to these there were three bins holding a hundredweight each of sugar, brown sugar, and flour. A smaller fourth bin held the salt. Another counter held a large roll of wrapping paper, a glass cheese case, and a bread case. At the end there was a very nice case for tobacco in tins or in bulk.

The right side of the store was the dry goods section, where boots and shoes could be found, along with men's clothing. In the middle of the store on the same counter were stationery supplies—pens and pencils, writing tablets, inks, and crayons—mingled with a few toys. Next there was a barrel of vinegar and a barrel of molasses, from which jugs could be filled as needed.

The center of the store held a display rack of cookies and crackers along with hardware such as lantern globes and boxes of bolts.

Mrs. Adams deliberately had the post office located at the back so that anyone entering to collect or send mail had to walk the length of the store and would hopefully see something that they needed or wanted to buy.

Next to the post office was a flight of stairs that led to the second floor—a single large room known as Adams Hall, which for decades had been used for social events such as weddings and dances. Just under the stairs there were two doors. One led out back and the other was the entrance to Mrs. Adams's home.

As was customary for the times, Mrs. Adams operated grocery wagons out of her store. For years her sons, Jake and Herman, both had routes making deliveries to farms in the surrounding countryside on a regular basis.

Years ago Benjamin began accompanying her boy Herman to learn the routes. It had been decided that it was time to train another person just in case one of her sons got sick or needed a day off. Benjamin proved to be quite reliable at learning the routes as well as understanding how to handle merchandise. Benjamin and Herman went out on a trip together to deliver a heavy anvil. It must have been on that trip that the boys picked up something catching. No one else in town got sick. Less than a week later both young men were dead. Mrs. Adams's grief was so severe that she missed both funerals.

At the jangle of her store bell, Mrs. Adams turned from her inventory list to see Natalie Cooper walking through the door, held open by Collin Bradley. "Miss Cooper, Mr. Bradley, welcome! If I can be of service, please don't hesitate to ask."

"Thank you, Mrs. Adams," they replied in unison. Looking at one another without comment, they parted for different areas of the store.

"Miss Cooper, you're wearing your red bonnet I see. So what is your Christmas mission for today?"

"I need to get some art supplies. I'm doing a few water-colors for presents this year."

"I have a selection over there at the middle counter. Follow me, and I will get them out for you. While you are making your choices, I will go and see if I can help Mr. Bradley. He is in back at the post office."

"Thank you, Mrs. Adams. I won't be but a moment."

As Mrs. Adams approached the back of the store, Collin produced a small package from inside his coat and said, "Here is the day's mail. Do you have anything for me to take back to the depot before the train leaves?"

Mrs. Adams produced a few letters and handed them to Collin.

"I'd better get these back now. I'm a little behind by time, and the train is due to leave shortly. I will come back later to fill my father's order."

Mrs. Adams said, "You can leave his list with me, and I will have everything ready for you when you return."

"Thank you, Mrs. Adams."

As Collin passed Natalie he said, teasingly, "Watch out for those highwaymen."

"Really, Collin!" she exclaimed.

Returning to help Natalie, Mrs. Adams remembered the first time she had noticed the girl. It was sometime after the funeral. Before that it had been Benjamin who had made the trips to the store for the family. After he died the task had fallen to Natalie. She had first come into the store to ask for something for her mother. As Natalie left the store that day, Mrs. Adams observed her straighten up the bars of soap. She had been quite incensed at the insult. Didn't that girl know that she was quite capable of taking care of her own store? This injury to Mrs. Adams's pride had been carried out every time Natalie came into the store, and for quite some time she didn't like seeing the girl come in.

Then one day she watched as Natalie came into the store to browse, and while she was browsing she went about straightening up anything at all that she supposed was out of place. She never once looked up to see who might be watching her. It was the absent-minded way that the girl was straightening things up that made Mrs. Adams realize she was only doing it to be helpful. Feeling suddenly remorseful and to test her theory she had said, "Natalie, thank you for helping me keep the store in order."

Natalie had looked up and said, "Oh, you're welcome. Mama says that if you see a thing that needs doing, you should just do it and save others the trouble."

"Well then," Mrs. Adams had replied, "I'm sure you have saved me quite a lot of trouble over the last few months." It was endearing how Natalie had reddened, a little embarrassed, and had fled the store. From then on Mrs. Adams was always delighted to have Natalie in the store, even if it was only to browse.

Turning her thoughts back to the present-day, Mrs. Adams inquired, "Are you finding what you need?"

Natalie stood there biting her lip a little before she answered. "Yes, thank you. I'm still trying to decide if I should purchase another brush. I'll take these colors, and I'll have eight sheets of this watercolor paper. I like its texture. . . ." She hesitated before adding, "and this brush."

With that Mrs. Adams wrapped up Natalie's purchase and sent her off, but not before the girl noticed something on the floor, bent down, picked it up, and deposited it in the dust bin. Mrs. Adams smiled.

November 16, 1881
A Dilemma

As Natalie awoke she found herself still pondering a dilemma from the previous night. She couldn't understand why she wanted to do what she had gotten into her head, but she did, and she couldn't get rid of her desire. She would ask her mother for her opinion. After dressing she made her way downstairs and into the kitchen.

"Mama, can I speak to you for a moment?"

"Yes, Natalie, what is it?"

"I have been reading the Nativity in Luke, and I find myself wanting to ask Bishop Versey if I can deliver it this year on Christmas Sunday."

Mrs. Cooper regarded her daughter. If this idea had come from anyone else other than Natalie, she would have answered with her first impulse: it was not a wise request for a young woman in a world where it was practically unheard of for a woman to deliver the gospel outside of her home. Natalie was more audacious, however, and in order to have more time to think she replied honestly, "I need time to consider. You get some breakfast."

It had always been either she or Natalie who had been interested in having the gospel in the Cooper household. Mr. Cooper was receptive but not interested in taking the lead where faith was concerned. She had come to know many a household in which it was the woman who made sure that Christ was in the home. So what harm would it do to ask? Why not have a woman deliver the Nativity? Personally, she liked the idea.

"I think that you should ask," she said to Natalie. "If anyone other than Bishop Versey were to deliver the Nativity, I would want it to be you. You always do it so beautifully here at home, and you are very well thought of by him, so there could be a chance."

"Oh thank you, Mama. I had hoped you would approve. I'll find just the right time to tell Papa. Do you think he will like the idea?"

"I think that you should wait until after you find out what the bishop says, and then make it known to your father," Mrs. Cooper advised. Then she added, "You have it memorized, don't you?"

Natalie nodded with a grin, and with that she helped with the rest of breakfast, cleaned up, and went off to continue her Christmas preparations.

Monday, November 28, 1881
The Request—Almost

It was on a Monday that Natalie headed for the church to make her Christmas request. She knew exactly how she was going to approach the bishop, and she hoped very much that he would be in favor of it.

Just as Natalie opened the door to the church, she heard a crash and the shattering of glass. She quietly peeked into the chapel and found Bishop Versey with his back to her. One of the candlesticks had smashed on the floor. There had been two of them—quite beautiful and made of crystal. Now there was only one.

Natalie decided not to ask the bishop her question just then. She would come back later. Backing quietly out of the church, she left unnoticed.

Tuesday, November 29, 1881
The Purchase

Lead crystal candlesticks were rather expensive and Natalie had no idea how Bishop Versey would replace it, with all the expenses of serving his flock at Christmas. Natalie had spent the night considering and deciding what she was going to do. She would dip into her savings and replace it herself.

When all of her chores were done, she changed clothes, put on her red bonnet, and left for the General Store.

Natalie was relieved to find that, for the moment, she was the only one there. She walked straight to Mrs. Adams. "Mrs. Adams, I have a request to make. It might sound strange, but would you happen to have any candlesticks similar to those found at the church?"

"No, not in stock, but we can look through a catalog and order them for you."

"Will it take long?"

"It depends on what you choose. Chances are your selection will be found at Overton's Mercantile in Newark. We could send a telegram to inquire. If Overton's has them, your selection can be put on the train and be here in no time at all."

"I would like to try."

Mrs. Adams found the right catalog, passed it to Natalie, and left her to page through it. Only minutes later Natalie found candlesticks that were very similar to the old ones.

"These here," she said, pointing to the page, "will do very nicely."

Mrs. Adams glanced at her choice and agreed. "If you have other errands in town, I can send an inquiry and then let you know what I find out. Stop by before you go home."

"That will be fine. I do have Christmas shopping to do both here and at the ladies' store. I'll linger a while there and then come back here."

Natalie had decided that Christelle was going to get a white bonnet from her this year. Natalie had caught her trying on her red bonnet, and seeing Christelle's disappointment at having to give it back gave her the idea. Mrs. Linden's ladies' store was the place to find it, so off she went.

At the store Mrs. Linden showed her some choices. Natalie selected one that she particularly liked and decided that, with a little of her own creativity, it would be perfect for Christelle. She made her purchase and returned to Mrs. Adams's store.

As Natalie entered, Mrs. Adams spied her and said, "I have good news for you. They have them in stock at Overton's Mercantile. Shall I place the order?"

"Yes, thank you."

"Very good. I will let you know when they come in."

"Thank you very much for all your trouble."

"Not at all, my dear, not at all. Good day, Natalie."

Having successfully achieved her goals, Natalie spent the rest of the day reading by the fireplace. *It's going to be such fun sneaking the candlesticks into the church,* she thought.

Wednesday, November 30, 1881
Christmas Presents

Natalie's favorite creature comfort in the whole world was to be warm. She thrived on warmth. If necessary, she would deal with the cold, but only so long as it was necessary. This year she decided that most of her Christmas presents would be centered around being warm.

Natalie retrieved a pair of her father's old gloves that he had tossed in the dust bin and used them as a pattern. Carefully she took them apart and reproduced new ones that she was sure would be warmer. Making her father's pair brought back fond memories of making the pair for Mr. Hope. This success gave her the desire to make a third pair for Bishop Versey.

For Mrs. Adams, she finished up a red shawl. Natalie thought she would like red because of how she emphasized "*red* bonnet" whenever she saw Natalie wearing it.

For her mother, she had spent the year secretly working on a quilt, spending time on it whenever her mother was away or late at night when the whole house was asleep. Now all she had to do was wrap it up.

Collin was going to get a scarf, which she hoped would be finished sometime around the fifteenth of December if she were going to stay on her schedule. She had made a number of scarves already for others in need, but she planned to make Collin's special by embroidering a little something on it to give him a clue of how fond she was of him. Now she just had to figure out what that would be.

That evening Natalie got out her watercolors and worked on the little paintings that she intended for her friends at school. She used her Currier and Ives print collection for inspiration. Natalie had started her collection after reading in the *American Woman's Home* that Currier and Ives prints were considered appropriate for a proper American home. The first print of her collection was called *Kiss Me Quick*. It reminded her of the time she heard her father say it to her mother just before they went into the dining room where family and friends were waiting to celebrate her mother's birthday. As Natalie collected each print, she stored them in a very large scrapbook. Though she had scattered a few valentines among the pages, the prints were her favorites. New prints led to new paintings, and new paintings led to the desire for new prints. She particularly enjoyed the snow scenes, especially the ones with a horse and a sleigh.

As the evening came to a close, Natalie tidied up and put everything away except for what she was going to need tomorrow. Pondering the reactions of how her gifts were going to be received made her smile. "Christmas is going to be such fun!" she exclaimed out loud to the Christmas spirits.

Thursday, December 1, 1881
The Lesson

One of Nathan Cooper's most cherished memories was of dancing with Clarice in their kitchen on a Christmas morning some years back. The only music playing was Clarice's sweet voice humming a little waltz that they both knew. It was a very precious way of loving her.

Today he was supposed to teach Natalie how to dance. She wanted to be prepared to go to the dance at Adams Hall on the fourteenth.

Natalie had been asked to the dance by Toby Tucker, but she wasn't sure she wanted to go with him. He was a nice enough young man, but she had hoped that someone else would ask, and so far he hadn't shown the nerve to do it. "You shall remain unnamed, *Mr. Collin Bradley,* but you had better hurry up and ask," she declared to herself. She couldn't leave Mr. Tucker in limbo much longer and would have to answer him soon. As Natalie finished getting dressed she let out a sigh of worry that she might have to go with Mr. Tucker. *Well I'd better get this over with.*

Natalie came to the parlor door in a very pretty blue dress. Mr. Cooper started to whistle but caught himself, thinking it improper that he should whistle at his own daughter. Instead he said, "My! Don't you look nice."

"Thanks, Papa. Mama helped me make it."

Mr. Cooper met her at the door and led her to the center of the floor. "I am not the best dancer, but I'll show you what I know, and that should get you through the dance well enough."

He placed her directly in front of him and demonstrated the proper position for doing the waltz. Next he showed her the basic steps and actually managed not to step on her toes. After a short while she was getting the rhythm of the waltz quite nicely.

Mrs. Cooper entered the room, helped Natalie to place her arms in a better position, and then sat down at the piano to play "The Blue Danube Waltz." Ever since she had learned this piece of music, it had become a favorite in the Cooper household.

Mr. Cooper had thought that Natalie would have learned to dance years ago, but for whatever reason, she had never shown interest in it as young ladies usually did.

For the first time in Natalie's life, she was in love with the idea of dancing. She never knew that it could be so much fun twirling around the room. Ever since her experience with sea sickness on the S. S. *Frisia,* she had been afraid of what dancing in circles might do to her, but today she was just fine and was having a glorious time. Natalie was determined to dance for the rest of her life.

"Papa, I could do this all night!"

"If you do, you won't have a papa as a partner, I assure you."

"Just a little longer—please, Papa?"

Mr. Cooper was now regretting how enthusiastic Natalie had become with waltzing around the room. By the time she let him stop he was so plum tuckered out that he could hardly make it to his chair to sit down. He was beginning to think that he never wanted to hear that waltz again, lovely as it was.

"That was glorious, Papa, just glorious!"

"I am glad you are happy. You will do just fine at the dance, should you choose to go."

Natalie swished her skirt side to side and replied, "Oh, I'm going to go to that dance even if I have to dance with Mr. Tucker." Then she began waltzing out of the room without a partner and declared, "I am now a dancer!"

Friday, December 2, 1881
Precious Time

Mrs. Cooper and Natalie sat together, surveying the coming morning from their front window while still in their night attire. It was a red sunrise, which just might be the precursor of a storm. Mrs. Cooper buttoned the collar of her modest and warm flannel nightgown around her neck. *There certainly was something appealing about wearing flannel,* she thought.

Mrs. Cooper felt that it was a good time to tell her daughter a little of what she had learned while being married to Mr. Cooper. "Natalie, since you are almost seventeen I want to share something with you that you will likely work out on your own, but if I tell you now, you will be able to take advantage of knowing it sooner."

"What is it, Mama?

"It is this: While being married to your father over these many years, I have discovered that we have actually spent very little time together. Looking further I realized that this was true for everyone I knew. We spend the vast majority of our lives alone with our own thoughts and away from others. Unless you are one of the few who is comfortable living this way, it is not healthy.

"All of my most precious memories are of those moments when I was spending time with your father or with you children, as well as with others I love. Close—together— like reading stories to you when you were little and now this morning before anyone else is up.

"Whomever you choose for a husband, give him as much of your time as you possibly can and in turn help him to understand this truth so that he gives his time back to you. Our time is all we really have to give that matters. Time is so precious because we have so very little of it. Understand?"

"Yes, Mama, I do."

"Good. I hope you will take it to heart, because I am convinced that you will have a happier life if you do."

"I will, Mama. I promise."

Silence ensued with neither Natalie nor her mother wanting to leave the moment behind. They sat holding hands in the quiet of the morning, lost in their own thoughts until they were interrupted by a little creak on the floor behind them. Turning, they saw that five-year-old Christelle was up, and now the day had to officially start.

Both mother and daughter got up together and made straight for the little girl, sweeping her up into the air. Christelle squealed with surprise and delight.

"Let's make breakfast together, shall we?" suggested Mrs. Cooper.

Saturday, December 3, 1881
The Candlesticks Arrive

Natalie awoke with excitement. This was the day that Mrs. Adams had told her to expect the candlesticks to arrive on the morning train. If they did, the timing would be perfect. Most everyone in town knew that on the first and third Saturdays of the month Bishop Versey stopped in at Rogers's Barbershop for a haircut.

Natalie had decided exactly how she was going to get the candlesticks into the church without anyone suspecting. Her mother had on occasion brought the bishop dinner in a large basket. It would more than accommodate the candlesticks. Just to be on the safe side, she would add some goodies to cover them.

This wouldn't be the first time someone had taken advantage of him being out to slip something into the church—and very likely not the last. If she were seen, it would appear as though she were simply on an errand for her mother.

At the appointed time Natalie stopped in at the store with anticipation. She was delighted to find the candlesticks waiting for her. Mrs. Adams lifted an eyebrow when she saw Natalie place them into the basket. Natalie lifted a finger to her mouth. "Shhhhhh," she warned and winked.

Surprised, Mrs. Adams said, "I see nothing; I know nothing."

Natalie deliberately walked passed the barber's to see if the bishop was in his usual place. She saw him and he saw her. Natalie simply smiled and kept walking on down the street. Her heart, however reacted differently: it started to beat very fast. Natalie realized that she actually had a chance to get the candlesticks delivered unnoticed. With each step her heart beat faster and by the time she reached the church, she felt like it was going to burst right out of her chest. When she reached the door she went right in.

It was customary for the doors to be unlocked. Bishop Versey wanted the church open and available as much as possible. The broken candlestick was still there, but it was no longer able to hold one third of the candles that it previously held. She couldn't decide what to do with the old candlesticks, so she simply placed them on the floor out of the way. Removing the new candlesticks from her basket, she carefully positioned them in their proper place. They looked lovely. She only hoped that the old ones didn't hold any sentimental value for anyone.

Natalie went boldly to the door and looked out. Luckily there was no one in sight. Retracing her steps, she walked back past the barbershop to the general store. She had decided to give Bishop Versey the goodies, but without the candlesticks the basket was mostly bare. She would add a few things before giving it to him.

Mrs. Adams saw that the basket was now empty of the candlesticks. "It looks like you have had success."

Natalie smiled mischievously, her eyes bright with excitement.

"Are you going to tell me what you've been up to, or am I going to have to find out for myself? I always do, you know."

"You're going to have to wait. I really like staying anonymous for as long as possible."

"I understand, Miss Cooper. Now what can I do for you?"

"I have some goodies to give to the bishop, and I need a few more things because what I have here underwhelms the basket," she said, holding it open for inspection.

"I see what you mean."

"I was thinking that since the bishop shops here, you would know what he likes."

"I do indeed. I can tell you that he likes spiced peaches and is fond of raisins, as well as most any fruit."

Mrs. Adams made selections and placed them into the basket until Natalie was satisfied.

"I think that will do nicely," Natalie concluded.

Just before she turned to leave, she heard Bishop Versey's voice behind her. She stiffened and her heart leapt up into her throat. She had to fight to get control of her emotions. Had she been seen? Was she caught?

"Good day, ladies. I have had a most wonderful surprise. Someone has taken it into their heart to replace my broken candlestick. They left behind a matched set so that the old one wouldn't look awkward with the new one!"

Both women feigned surprise. "I wonder who it could have been," said Mrs. Adams, sweeping her gaze from Natalie's face to the bishop's.

Natalie, not realizing that she had been holding her breath, exhaled in relief. She had been counting on Mrs. Adams to keep her secret.

"For the life of me I don't know," replied the bishop. "I broke it on Monday, and as far as I can tell, no one has even been inside the church to know that it was broken. I've been there almost every moment since making repairs and getting ready for Christmas. It's quite a mystery."

"Well, the Lord doth provide," said Mrs. Adams.

Natalie's heart began to beat fast. She was just a little embarrassed that her gift had been discovered so quickly. Changing the subject, she said to the bishop, "Mother and I have a few things here for you. We hope that you can use them." She handed the basket to the bishop and began to leave. "I will come for the basket later," she called over her shoulder. "I am behind my time and need to hurry off." With that, Natalie made a hasty exit.

"The Lord doth provide," repeated Mrs. Adams to the bishop with a deep feeling in her heart of how lucky they were to have Natalie Cooper.

The bishop responded, "Yes indeed, and sometimes twice in the same day."

"Well, Bishop, what can I do for you?"

"I came by to get a few things," he said while peering into the basket, "but now it seems I am quite well taken care of."

"Yes it does," agreed Mrs. Adams.

"Good day, Mrs. Adams."

"Good day, Bishop."

Sunday, December 4, 1881
Nativity

Natalie sat in the parlor wearing her red bonnet and holding a green and red wooden box that contained her favorite part of Christmas. When she was younger she would eagerly watch Benjamin gently remove and set up the Nativity. Now the Nativity was her responsibility. Though Natalie loved handling and placing the pieces, she wished with all her heart that Benjamin was there to do it. This year Christelle was old enough to help her.

"Christelle!" called Natalie. "Where are you?"

She heard the voice of her little sister say, "Coming!" and a moment later Christelle skipped into the parlor.

"Do you know what today is?" Natalie asked her.

"Sunday?"

"Yes, Sunday. But this is a very special Sunday."

"Why?"

"It is the first Sunday in December, and that is the day that we set up our Nativity for Christmas. This has been a Cooper tradition since before I was born. I will open the box and you can take the pieces out, but you have to be very careful not to break anything. Do you think you can do that?"

Christelle nodded with eager anticipation.

Their Nativity had been made in France by her mother's grandfather, who was a master woodcarver. He was in high demand in Bordeaux, and his masterpieces could be found all over the city. Mrs. Cooper had been given this set as a little girl. He had carved it for himself and later gave it to her after he had replaced it with another one more to his liking. Mrs. Cooper, for the life of her, couldn't find anything at all wrong with this one, except that it was very old with crackling paint and some worn edges. She had concluded that it was her grandfather's way of passing on the tradition.

Each figure was carefully wrapped in strips of white cloth. When all of the figures had been removed and unwrapped, the girls decided where to put them. Natalie coaxed Christelle into placing the manger where the sun would hit it in the early evenings, making the Nativity glow as if the Christ child were really there. She promised her little sister that she would not be disappointed.

Mrs. Cooper had taught Natalie that the first Nativity was created by St. Francis of Assisi. He was concerned that the meaning of Christmas was becoming lost, so taking advantage of a nearby cave in Greccio, Italy, he set about using real people and animals for a living Nativity.

After the manger was placed, Natalie showed Christelle where the baby Jesus would later rest. "Right here in the middle," she pointed. "Next, Mary is placed so that she will be looking lovingly over her son. Joseph is next, and then we add the Star of Bethlehem. We also have the angel Gabriel, shepherds, and the wisemen. I like putting this baby lamb near where Baby Jesus will be because he was called the Lamb of God."

Christelle asked, "Why don't we put in the baby Jesus now?"

"We wait until Christmas Eve because he has not been born yet. So we set him nearby."

"But I want him to be with his mother now," she insisted.

"He will be—very soon. We must be patient," replied Natalie.

With the last piece in place, the girls called for their mother to come give her approval.

"Very nice," said Mrs. Cooper. "I think this is the best it has ever looked."

Christelle beamed with joy and, just as she had entered, went skipping out of the parlor, off to play.

Natalie and her mother sat admiring the beginnings of Christmas in the Cooper home.

Monday, December 5, 1881
Ornaments

Every year the Cooper household spent an entire day making Christmas ornaments. Mrs. Cooper decided that this year they would make them early enough to mail them in time for relatives to receive them before Christmas instead of after.

Natalie had a favorite ornament that she always looked forward to making: golden wishbones. Over the course of the year she saved all of the chicken wishbones that she could. This year she was surprised to find that she had fifty-two, one for each week of the year. She never needed that many and used only the best for Christmas presents. The rest would be for fun—for breaking with family and friends whenever the occasion presented itself.

Even before she started saving them for ornaments, Natalie very much enjoyed the tradition of breaking the wishbone and the person with the longer piece being granted a wish. She could never remember getting her wishes unless she happened to wish for something that was almost certain to happen anyway. She found much more happiness in losing the break so that others could have a wish. Natalie often shared the wishbones for birthdays, trying her best to make sure that the birthday recipient won the break. It was fun pretending to be upset with losing so the winner could feel more victorious.

This Christmas Natalie needed twenty-five wishbones. She would make four sets of six to give as gifts, and she traditionally made one wishbone for her family and added it to the tree. This year's addition would make . . . *Let's see,* she thought, *number seven—a lucky number!*

At that moment Mrs. Cooper came over and presented Natalie with a very large wishbone. "I've been saving this for you. It's from one of the geese we had a while back."

Natalie happily accepted it, declaring, "It's going to be this year's addition to the family collection."

Looking over her assortment, Natalie started by selecting the wishbones with the best shape. Next she tried to create matched sets by having each wishbone in the set be as close to the same size as possible. She carefully wrapped them in whisper-thin gold foil, finishing them off with matching ribbons so they could be hung from the tree. She loved the idea of giving away wishes.

After she finished Natalie decided that she and Christelle would break one of the extra wishbones. She would try to make sure that Christelle won, and if she didn't, there was always the tradition of being able to present the winning part to another person, thereby transferring the wish. Ever since she had begun this as a Christmas tradition, she had never kept a single wish for herself. It was just too much fun giving them away.

Later that evening Christelle ran happily around the house declaring, "I won! I won! I won! I get my wish!"

Tuesday, December 6, 1881
Flowers

Natalie needed to stop in at the General Store for some extra sugar. As she entered, an array of bright red flowers stopped her in her tracks. "Flowers in December!" she exclaimed in surprise.

"Aren't they beautiful?" remarked Mrs. Adams. "A Mrs. Enteman and her daughter brought them by. They are growing them in their greenhouses and are hoping they will catch on."

"They are lovely! I would like to have that one for my mother," said Natalie pointing to a plant thick with blooms.

"They are rather expensive."

"Are they?"

"The price of that new dress you planned on buying," remarked Mrs. Adams.

"Oh my, that much? It seems as though I have a dilemma." Natalie sat pondering what to do while she stared at the flowers. Breaking her silence she asked, "What are they called?"

"Mrs. Enteman calls it a poinsettia. She also said that its scientific name, which I can't remember for the life of me, means 'very beautiful.'"

"They are indeed," agreed Natalie. "The dress is going to have to wait. I want my mother to have a poinsettia. I will come back for it later. Right now I need some sugar, and I can't carry both."

"That will be fine. Mrs. Enteman said they are sensitive to the cold, so it will need to be covered before you take it home." Mrs. Adams put Natalie's sugar order on the counter. "You live close enough that it should be fine," she speculated.

"I will pay for it now so that I don't lose it to someone else, and I'll come back in the morning."

"Very good, I'll be happy to hold it for you."

Natalie finished her transaction and turned to leave.

"See you in the morning!" Mrs. Adams called after her.

"See you first thing in the morning, Mrs. Adams, and thank you."

Wednesday, December 7, 1881
Afternoon Skating Party

Though there was no snow yet, Natalie was grateful that it had been cold enough to create a layer of ice on Johnson Pond thick enough for the annual ice skating party. It was a very large pond surrounded by starkly barren trees that were interrupted by Mr. Johnson's newly painted red barn. Why red she didn't know, but she thought that it looked quite nice.

This was an important annual event, so the town of Chester hired professional musicians to come all the way from Montclair. There were tables of food and several fires going to provide warmth.

A great many folk showed up for the festivities—some from out of town. The girls were dressed in yellows, pinks, and greens, looking more like an Easter assemblage than a Christmas one. Natalie disrupted this group of color by dressing in all red to match her bonnet since this was a Christmas event.

She didn't know how she and Collin had managed it, but over the years they had never been to the skating party at the same time. She found herself looking forward to seeing him, and she hoped that they would have time for a skate together.

Upon seeing Natalie, Collin's heart beat faster. He dearly hoped that she would consent to at least one skate with him— if he could get up the courage to ask her. He prayed silently for it to happen.

Many people were skating. Some skaters looked as though they had wings and were intoxicated by the freedom of the ice. For those who could not skate and still wanted to enjoy the ice, skating chairs were available. They were often occupied by wives or girlfriends and pushed by their companions. Sometimes a skating chair was occupied by an old man who seemed to revel in being out on the ice. With the exception of the normal falls, bumps, and bruises, everyone enjoyed themselves.

During the games of tag, Natalie observed that Collin spent a great deal of time helping others back to their feet. Losing hope for a skate with him, she decided she was going to have to make him come to her. A little while later she saw her chance.

Collin had gathered a group of skaters for a game of crack the whip and was skating around as the lead. With determination, Natalie began skating as hard as she could around the edge of the ice. Unobserved by Collin, she reached out at just the right moment and boldly took the hand of Debbie Tober who was at the end of the whip. Natalie felt exhilarated as she was pulled into the momentum of the game. Almost immediately, however, Collin reversed direction to crack the whip. He looked behind him to observe the results just in time to watch in horror as Natalie, Miss Tober, and another boy, went flying, all headed for different parts of the pond. Natalie was tripped up by a skater in her path, which sat her down with her skirt in a perfect circle, spinning like a top.

Collin broke free and quickly skated to her.

With great concern he asked, "Are you all right, Miss Cooper?" He wanted to say "sweetheart," but the word was just too shy to come out.

"Yes, quite, Mr. Bradley."

Collin stood there with his hands on his knees, trying to catch his breath.

"Are you going to help me up like those little rascals that you have been saving all day, or are you going to just stand there gaping?"

"Yes, certainly, Miss Cooper."

"Well, which is it, helping or gaping?"

"Uh—helping," replied Collin, extending a hand.

"It's about time!" Natalie scolded. "I'm starting to freeze in places that have never before felt such cold!"

It was difficult to get traction, so Collin needed two hands to pull Natalie to her feet. He didn't know if it was by accident or on purpose, but she stumbled ever so slightly, and before he knew it, the space between them evaporated. And there she was, where he had always wanted her—in his arms. Her breath, steamy in the frosty air, mingled with her perfume. A fragrance that he couldn't place became treasured, forever secure in his memory. He lingered only a moment longer than he should have and then said softly, "Miss Cooper, whatever possessed you to become the end of the whip?"

Breathless in Collin's embrace, Natalie managed to answer, "I have watched the game numerous times and thought that it would be fun. I was just fine until I was tripped up."

"You were indeed," agreed Collin. "Miss Cooper, the next time you decide to become the end of the whip, would you please make sure that I am not the one to send you flying off hither and yon?"

Exploring her eyes, Collin considered kissing her, but his courage fled when she replied, "Mr. Bradley, I do believe you care."

"I need to help Tad. He's over there," Collin said quickly, while breaking away.

Natalie turned to see little Tad Johnson face down on the ice in tears, hatless and struggling to get up. Collin skated swiftly over. He helped the boy up, brushed him off, replaced his hat, and wiped away the tears. Then, to her surprise, Collin gave Tad a reassuring hug and sent the youngster happily on his way. Collin's gentleness completely melted Natalie's heart. In that moment her heart became Collin's, without him even knowing it.

❈ ❈ ❈

Natalie arrived home, her eyes bright and her pink cheeks aglow.

Her father looked up from repairing a favorite chair. "You look like you've had a good time."

"I have, Papa."

"What is it? Some young gentleman catch your fancy?" he teased. When Natalie nodded, He dropped his tack hammer and stood up. She had his attention. "Who, might I ask?"

"Collin."

"Collin Bradley? I don't think he quite measures up, if you know what I mean."

"That has never bothered me, Papa."

"Why Collin? You've known the young man for years, and I've never seen you show any interest."

"I have always been interested in Collin. I have been careful not to show it, just in case he turned out to be different than I supposed. Today I confirmed exactly who he is."

"What do you mean?"

"Papa, he's not only a gentleman, he's a gentle man. I've seen it."

Mr. Cooper observed by Natalie's gaze that she was somewhere far away and no longer with him. After a moment she continued, "Papa, I know what is in his heart, and I want it."

"You like the young man, then?"

"I love him, Papa."

"Quite remarkable." Her father paused for a moment, considering what to say. What was there to say? Natalie had always shown restraint. He couldn't ever remember her being hasty, and now she had declared her love for Collin. "I can see that your mind is made up, so I choose to support you. He's going to be the luckiest man on the face of the earth—next to me, of course, since I have had the pleasure of being your father and married to your mother," he mused with satisfaction. "Tell me: how do you plan to let him know that he is to be yours?"

"When he sees that he is the only gentleman to whom I will show my affection, he will get the idea rather quickly, I think. Isn't that how Mama won you?"

"Yes indeed. He doesn't have a chance of escaping. You know, your mother and I have always liked young Mr. Bradley, as well as his family. Natalie?"

"Yes, Papa?"

"I've noticed that Collin has been devoted to you for years."

Natalie nodded, bounced up to her father, planted a kiss on his cheek. "Who is going to tell Mama?"

"You can. Run along and convey my approval. I am confident that she will take it well."

Natalie radiantly waltzed out of the room with an invisible Collin in her arms. As she left she stopped suddenly remembering, Mr. Tucker's invitation to the dance. Natalie's mind was made up. "Well, Mr. Tucker, I am going to have to decline your offer to the dance since this very day I have given my heart to Collin." She said quietly to herself, "I will even suffer not going to the dance if I have to, though I do hope Collin will hurry up and ask me. I may have to drop an obvious hint."

Thursday, December 8, 1881
The Request

Bishop Versey exited the church on his way to purchase new candles for the sacrament. Looking up, he made note of the overcast sky and then became aware of Miss Cooper's approach. She was headed directly toward him or so it appeared. She had a very determined look on her face, as if she were on a mission. He stopped walking the moment he was sure that he was her intended destination.

"Miss Cooper, good afternoon."

"Good afternoon, Bishop." Then, before she could decide otherwise, she blurted out softly, "I have a request to make of you regarding the program on Christmas Sunday."

"Pray, continue." Bishop Versey's countenance changed suddenly from curiosity to awe. He didn't know how it had happened, but at that moment Miss Cooper seemed to be bathed in a pool of light, as if the sun had moved directly over her. Her hair and skin shown with a luminous clarity for a few beautiful moments, and then it was lost. Glancing up he could see no opening among the gray clouds.

Natalie gave a little shrug. "Maybe I am overstepping my bounds, but I would very much like to read the Christmas story in Luke this year." She looked up expectantly. "I would do it well for you."

Bishop Versey was touched. "I know you would, Miss Cooper. The idea is not unfavorable to me personally, but I think that it would be for others. There are some in the congregation who would likely look with disfavor at not having their bishop perform his duty—especially at Christmastime."

Seeing the disappointment on her face, he immediately added, "However, I will give it serious thought, along with some prayer, and let you know later. Does that meet with your approval?"

"Oh yes! Thank you." Her hope had returned, and Bishop Versey was relieved to have more time to ponder the matter.

"Good day, Miss Cooper."

"Good day, Bishop."

❄ ❄ ❄

When Bishop Versey returned to the chapel with the candles, he did not delay his inquiry to God regarding Natalie's wish. When he rose from his knees, he felt much better about letting her read Luke this year. It would be a nice change to approach the Christmas program differently. He would pass it by Mrs. Messing. If he could get her support, then the others on the church board would likely support him as well. Mrs. Messing had proved to be very influential and he had learned early on that she was often his biggest hurdle.

Later, at her home, Mrs. Messing was in a perfect fury. "Certainly not, Bishop. I am completely against having Miss

Cooper read the Nativity. That is your responsibility. How would it look to have this young woman up there doing your job? I cannot support it."

"I only thought . . ."

"No, you didn't think," she interrupted. "You have been charged by us with bringing the gospel to the good people of Chester, and we expect *you* to do it. I also expect you to tell the Cooper girl to get this absurd idea completely out of that head of hers and to not let it back in. I am sorry, Bishop, but we want you to do it the same as you always have."

"Very well, Mrs. Messing," said Bishop Versey's lips, though he was thinking "Mrs. Mess-It-Up." He turned to go and added, "I will let Miss Cooper know. Good day, Mrs. Messing"

❊ ❊ ❊

In order to keep the peace with Mrs. Messing, Bishop Versey told Natalie the truth. Though deeply disappointed, she did, however, understand his position.

"Some day a lady is going to stand up in church and preach the gospel without judgment or disapproval," she said with foresight.

"I believe you are right, Miss Cooper."

With that, the painful matter was finished, and Bishop Versey watched Natalie leave. For the first time in as long as he could remember she left without smiling.

Friday, December 9, 1881
Carols with Christelle

Natalie and Christelle sat in the parlor watching the last rays of the sun play across the Nativity. "You were right, Natalie. It looks just like the Star of Bethanyham, just like you said."

"That's *Bethlehem*," Natalie corrected absentmindedly. *Bethany would make a nice girl's name,* she thought, remembering that Bethany was the biblical village where Mary, Martha, and Lazarus had lived. She recalled Bishop Versey mentioning that some thought it was from Bethany that Jesus parted from his disciples at the ascension. Natalie decided to tuck the name away in her mind for future use.

"Would you like me to sing Christmas carols with you, Christelle? You said just last night that we haven't sung any yet and that you were missing them."

"Yes, please."

"How many should we sing?"

"Six!"

"Six? That's quite a lot if we sing all of the verses. I will agree only if we sing the first two verses of each. Then we can save the rest for later."

Natalie called, "Mama, Can you come play the piano for us?"

"Yes, I'll be there in a moment," Mrs. Cooper called from the kitchen.

Natalie could play, but not as well as her mother. When it came to playing the carols, her mother could almost do it blindfolded, and besides, it was much more fun to have their mother sing with them. The sweet harmonies of the trio would often bring Mr. Cooper running to the parlor. He was not at home, however, and would likely miss this round of carols.

First they sang "Angels We Have Heard on High," then "Deck the Hall," followed by "I Saw Three Ships" and "It Came upon the Midnight Clear." They finished with Christelle's favorite, "Jingle Bells," and with Natalie's favorite, "Joy to the World." By the time they sang the last note, their hearts were full of the Christmas spirit.

When they were finished Natalie suggested that they read something together. Mrs. Cooper excused herself, saying she had to check on her baking. Christelle chose her new book that was about Santa Claus. Natalie, while she loved dear old Santa, preferred to keep Christmas centered on Christ during the holiday. At that moment a thought popped into her head, and she decided to tell Christelle about her name. It had just occurred to Natalie that their mother had never told her sister why she was named Christelle, and with her now being five years old, she just might understand. Natalie had asked about it when Christelle was born, and she thought it was special.

"Christelle, my little sister, I have a question for you. Has Mama ever told you why she named you Christelle?"

"Not that I 'member."

"*Re*-member," Natalie gently corrected.

"Not that I *re*-member."

"Mama told me that throughout her life, whenever she was remembering Christ she was very much happier. So she decided that whether you were born a girl or a boy, you would have Christ in your name. When she saw that you were a beautiful baby girl, she was delighted to name you Christelle. So now we have you as a little reminder of Christ. You," she said, tapping her sister on the nose, "are named after the Savior of the world."

Christelle's eyes got very big. "I am?"

"You most certainly are!"

"Can you read my Santa book now?"

"Yes, of course, but only if you promise to run and tell Mama who you are named after when we're done. I think that it would make her very happy. Can you do that for me?"

Christelle looked up at her big sister and nodded her head solemnly.

Natalie began: "A visit from Saint Nicolas . . ."

Saturday, December 10, 1881
The Christmas Tree

Mrs. Cooper's goal was to make every Christmas tree more artistic than the year before. This year, however, the task fell to Natalie and Mr. Cooper because Christelle had become ill that very morning and was in need of her mother's attention.

"Natalie, your father has gone to get the tree. Could you please get out the ornaments? I'm not going to be any help. I'll be up with Christelle until I know how sick she is."

"Yes, Mama, right away. Do you need any help with Christelle?"

"I'll be all right, thank you. I'm going upstairs now. You and your father have a good time. We might be down later."

"We will, Mama. Tell Christelle I will miss her help."

A little while later Mr. Cooper came marching into the drawing room holding the little Christmas tree like it was a medieval standard, straight up with his arms extended out in front. "Ta-da," he said as Natalie looked up.

"Oh, Papa, where did you find it?"

"Out back, up on the hill. It has been waiting for some years now to become a Christmas tree for us. I noticed it when you were about ten or eleven, and since it has grown into such a fine shape, I decided that it should be this year's Christmas tree."

Gingerly he placed the evergreen into the tree stand while Natalie secured it.

"I see you've been getting the decorations ready. Shall we start?"

"Yes, please!"

"While you unwrap the ornaments, I will attach the candleholders." Mr. Cooper always performed this important task because, in his words, "it is my sacred responsibility to see that my family stays safe." When lit, the tree had to be tended at all times.

Next, the tree was loosely draped with strings of glass beads and then bedecked with an eclectic group of ornaments—several made by the family and others purchased by Mr. Cooper when on his occasional trips out of town.

The family ritual of placing the ornaments always started with one in particular that was stored in a little wooden box. The box was always opened by Mr. Cooper. The ornament was always given a place of honor on the tree by Mr. Cooper. And it was always removed from the tree and returned to the box by Mr. Cooper.

This Christmas ornament was the most cherished object that Nathan Cooper owned in the whole world. He was told that it had been given to him by his father. It was his only connection to him. Mr. Cooper called the ornament his Star of Bethlehem. This year he hung it high near the top of the tree and then made his yearly wish that one day he might find his father.

That was why he had come to America—to find his father. Mrs. Cooper, who had raised him, was the only parent he had ever known. She had told him his father lived in New Jersey in America, and that was why he ended up in Chester. He had not found his father, but he had found Clarice, and if that were all that ever happened from his coming to America, he would die happy, though not entirely content.

After the ornaments were in place, Natalie and her father delicately added the finishing touches: strands of shiny tinsel. The two of them stood back and admired their handiwork.

"There's nothing like a Christmas tree, Papa."

"Nothing like it," he agreed.

"Let's go and get Mama and Christelle to see the tree!"

"Yes, let's!"

Mr. Cooper carried Christelle into the drawing room. Wrapped up in a colorful quilt, she looked like a gift. After setting Christelle down on the sofa, Mr. Cooper began lighting the candles, and he asked Mrs. Cooper how she liked the tree.

"It's a little sparse here and there," she said pointing to several places on the tree.

"Oh, Mama, that's because we saved some of Christelle's favorite ornaments for her to put on the tree when she is well," Natalie explained. Turning to Christelle, she added with a whisper, "I also saved all of the golden wishbones for you."

"That was very thoughtful of you, Natalie," said Mrs. Cooper. "Christelle can look forward to doing her part, and the tree will be perfect."

Christelle, as sick as she was, managed a smile when her father finished lighting the candles. They all sat together admiring the tree until the fire started to die down. Mr. Cooper got up, revived the fire, and then gently lifted Christelle from the sofa. Natalie and Mrs. Cooper lovingly kissed Christelle high on her forehead before he carried her back upstairs.

"Get well quickly, my little one, so you can finish the tree and we can put up our stockings," he told her as he tucked her in. He added his goodnight kiss to her mother's and sister's.

Sunday, December 11, 1881
Going for Mistletoe on the Black River

Mr. Cooper entered the kitchen the next morning to find Natalie already there.

"Good morning, Papa."

"Good morning, Natalie. Up early aren't we?"

"Yes, a little," she replied. "I'm off to find mistletoe before services."

"For?"

"Collin," she admitted.

"Where will you be?"

"I'm going to search along the banks of the Black River. That's where the largest bunches are."

"How long will you be out?"

"An hour," she responded. "Maybe an hour and a half at the most."

Kissing her on the cheek, he said, "I'm off to make some morning deliveries. I'll see you when we both get back. It will be just you and I going to church. Christelle is still ill and mother will stay home with her." As he lifted his duster off its hook, he turned back and added, "Don't dally."

"I won't. I promise, Papa," she assured him just before the door closed with a little bang.

Natalie was dressed in a white jacket and a long ankle-length skirt, to which she added white leggings. All that she needed now was to put on her brown long coat and scarf, her mittens, and her red bonnet to be ready for her day out in the cold. Anticipation was welling up inside of her. She was looking forward to finding mistletoe and to the possibilities of what might happen later. Kissing Collin was a long-held desire, and since he was moving at glacial speed, she hoped the mistletoe would help things melt and move a little faster.

Small skiffs of snow lay in gentle billows against the door, wisping away as she opened it. She was looking forward to a real snow. The cold met her square in the face as she rewrapped her scarf around her neck. She faced it gladly, knowing that getting the mistletoe would be worth the inconvenience of enduring a little cold air.

Natalie kicked playfully through drifts of golden leaves, which crackled underfoot. The wind played an autumn song as it picked them up and played with them. The fall season was by far her favorite. She was just a little sad that it was nearing the end. This year's colors had been especially vibrant. Moments later she noticed the scent of snow in the wind. It was coming soon; she had better hurry.

About a mile from home Natalie began scanning the canopy for the perfect mistletoe—fresh and green—and she was surprised to find that here it had snowed about two inches. There was nothing back at the mill. For the first time in her life she realized that storms had edges to them.

Natalie continued her quest. She was determined to be successful, even though her errand was taking longer than she had planned. Just before she was ready to give up, she found herself standing near the river and a large tree looking up at what might be the perfect mistletoe. Adding to her delight, large, billowy snowflakes began drifting lazily down, landing on her upturned face. She opened her mouth and attempted to catch a few, then realized she was dallying.

"I guess I'm going to have to climb this tree if I want that mistletoe," she said aloud. Benjamin had taught her how to climb trees, and more important, how to get back down. She found it great fun to survey the world from the canopy of a tree. But this was going to be a short climb.

"I don't want to snag my bonnet," she said as she removed it and tied it over a low branch.

Natalie reached her goal in less than a minute and was pleased to see that up close the mistletoe was every bit as nice as it looked from the ground. She was making her selection when a sound like thunder echoed through the trees. As she glanced around looking for the source, she spied a perfect piece of mistletoe that was just within reach. She quickly picked it and gently tucked it inside her coat. As she climbed down she noticed the falling snow was no longer lazy and billowy but heavy and thick.

Natalie jumped lightly to the ground and reached for her bonnet. But she never touched it. Something large struck her from behind without warning, and she found herself falling down the embankment. Just as her mind began to comprehend what had happened, her head struck a rock and her world went instantaneously black. Limp and unconscious, she slid like a rag doll down the bank and onto the iced-over river.

Some moments later a loud pop rang through the still air, falling on deaf ears. The ice began crazing, cracking, and splitting underneath the prostrate body of the girl. Moments later the ice lost the struggle to support her, and Natalie was gone, swept under the ice by the current.

❄ ❄ ❄

Finished with his morning deliveries, Mr. Cooper stopped on the porch to stomp his boots and shake the snow off his coat. The most wonderful smell surrounded him, and his mouth began to water before he even went through the door. Mrs. Cooper was at the stove, and he stepped up behind her.

"Good morning again, my sweet wife." He kissed her on the cheek and looked over her shoulder. "Bacon! When?"

"It will be ready in just a few minutes," she said, lightly slapping away his anxious hand. "I've just put a kettle on for ginger tea. You can wait." She turned the bacon over in the pan. "That sure was a terrible squall we had this morning."

"Yes, it was. Did Natalie miss it?"

"Miss it? She's not with you?"

"She's not back?" Mr. Cooper was alarmed.

"Back? I thought she went with you. She's not here!" Mrs. Cooper saw him stiffen, and she did the same. She felt panic begin to set in.

"She left early to pick mistletoe, hoping to use it should Collin call. What time is it?"

"Nearly eleven."

Mr. Cooper calculated. "She's been gone three hours— twice as long as she expected to be. She's in trouble!" Bacon was now the furthest thing from his mind.

Mrs. Cooper, fearing for her daughter, paled and collapsed onto a chair.

The knock at the kitchen door interrupted their alarm. Nathan hurried to open it and found Collin standing there.

"Good morning, Mr. Cooper. I've brought over an early Christmas present for Miss Cooper and your family." He held up a nice looking ham and another little package. "Is she here? I'm also hoping to ask her to the dance."

"No, she's not here. We are quite concerned about her. She may be lost!"

Collin blew by him into the kitchen on a gale of cold air. "Where do you want me to start?"

"She was going to look for mistletoe along the banks of the Black River," Mr. Cooper quickly explained as he put on his coat. "I don't know which way she went, so we will have to split up. You go north—upstream—and I'll go south." Then he added, "She said that she was going to search along the banks of the river, so keep to the banks."

"Oh, please, God, let my little girl be all right," Mrs. Cooper sobbed as she watched the men rush out into the cold.

Mr. Cooper was surprised at how fast he could still run, even in the snow. If Natalie was hurt, she wouldn't last long in the snow and the cold. If more snow were to come, he might not find her at all. Time was the enemy, so he ran. After searching for nearly two hours and finding no sign of her, he prayed that Collin had found her. The journey back home was agony.

❄ ❄ ❄

Collin ran. Natalie was his joy. *No, she is more than that,* he thought. Suddenly Collin was overcome with the realization that, *not only was she his joy but she was his love. Why hadn't he shown it? That was going to change—and very soon!*

It was difficult to keep up the pace, but Collin pushed himself. He only stopped to rest when his lungs began burning, and then he continued as quickly as possible. After about an hour of long runs and short rests, his legs began to give out and he fell to his knees in the snow.

"I need to find her! I won't stop until I do!" Fighting back his fears, Collin pushed himself to his feet, and scanned the woods in all directions while he caught his breath. *There! What is that?* A speck of red stood out against the white snow. With renewed strength he rushed to it. It was Natalie's bonnet! He took it off the branch, instinctively brushing off the snow. *Natalie wouldn't like snow on her bonnet. Where . . . is . . . she?*

His gaze turned to the frozen river, riveting on a big ugly hole in the ice, which was near a snow-covered lump too small to be Natalie. Fear and emptiness struck like lightening, followed by thundering anguish knifing through his heart. He couldn't breathe. The blood drained from his head. Falling to his knees, dizzy and wracked with the sudden grief of loss, Collin cried out loud, "Natalie has drowned!" He gasped for breath between sobs. "She is dead and I am alive. This has . . . happened . . . to . . . the wrong person!" He screamed out loud.

Panic brought him back to his feet. With her bonnet clenched in his hand, he raced along the river searching frantically for her downstream, stopping at all the open water where the current was swift. His world was shattered. He wondered how he could live without her. The answer was that he couldn't.

Collin somehow made it back to the Coopers' house, arriving worn out and breathless. Mr. Cooper was on the porch preparing to go look for him. He ran across the yard, catching Collin just as he stumbled. Collin lifted his face. Their eyes met, and the grief in Collin's gaze was unmistakable. Mr. Cooper steeled himself for what Collin had to say.

"What have you found?"

In his misery Collin blurted out, "She's drowned, sir!" Collin stood like a blind man, seeing nothing before him, lost in a memory of Natalie. Not wanting to believe his own words, his thoughts were in confusion. Finding a voice not quite his own, he continued, "I found her bonnet hanging from a tree next to the river. There is a large hole in the ice where she has fallen through. I searched far downstream, and . . . and there is no sign of her," he ended with a sob.

The pain and despair that Nathan Cooper had known from Benjamin's death instantly flooded his soul. Burning tears filled his eyes and he blinked madly, struggling to think. Regaining some composure, he shook Collin by the shoulders and with a voice hoarse with grief managed to say, "Run to town. Find Constable Mallory and get help. Bring him back here, and then you can take us there."

Still clutching Natalie's red bonnet, Collin turned and hurried to town with what strength he had left.

Head down and shoulders sagging under the weight of his grief, Nathan turned to go and tell Clarice the terrible news about their sweet daughter. He was going to have to stay by her side for a very long time, and someone would need to be fetched to care for Christelle.

The moment Mr. Cooper entered the room with his frozen stare, Mrs. Cooper knew that it had happened again. She jumped up and screamed. Her husband came to her and she found refuge in his arms. The appalling weight of the sorrow she carried inside from the death of her beloved Benjamin was now compounded with the loss of Natalie. In a complete panic, she felt she needed to have Christelle safe in her arms or she would go mad. She ran upstairs and scooped Christelle into her arms. "My baby, my baby, my babies, my babies," she wailed. Christelle, not understanding what was wrong, cried with her mother.

❄ ❄ ❄

When Collin entered the General Store, there were three people standing by the wood stove warming themselves and chatting. They were still dressed from church services. One was a man that Collin did not know. The others were Mrs. Adams and Mr. Kincannon, a pleasant man who had some-times filled in at the school for Mrs. Trubl. Mrs. Adams, seeing the expression of pain and despair on Collin's face and the familiar red bonnet in his hand, asked, "What has happened, Collin?"

"Natalie Cooper has drowned!"

"What?" shrieked Mrs. Adams in her little voice.

"She drowned out on the Black River. It looks like she fell while trying to gather mistletoe. I found her bonnet, and there's a big hole in the ice. I'm looking for Constable Mallory to let him know. Have any of you seen him?"

All three shook their heads in unison.

"Can I help?" asked Mr. Kincannon.

"I don't know," replied Collin. "We have to find her body. It could be anywhere down river."

After Collin left, the three recipients of this tragic news fell into three kinds of morose silence—sympathetic, stunned, and depressed. Mrs. Adams tried to keep her broken heart from bursting, but she couldn't and began to cry. Mr. Kincannon wrapped his arms around the old woman and let her weep on his shoulder as the other man stood quietly, shaking his head sadly at the news of this poor girl whom he did not even know.

❄ ❄ ❄

By three o'clock that afternoon the entire town of Chester had learned of the death of one of their most cherished citizens. The news had spread like a wildfire, and Constable Mallory had gathered volunteers to look for the girl.

Mrs. Viola Messing took the news harder than most. Why hadn't she wanted the girl to read the Nativity? Natalie Cooper was so much like she had been when she was young, but Mrs. Messing had turned out to be a bitter old woman. Natalie Cooper had taken an entirely different path and had become a vibrant young woman whom everybody loved. The actual truth was plain: she was jealous of the girl. Natalie had had the moxie to ask the bishop to read the Nativity, thinking that a woman could actually do it. And why not? If anyone could have done it, it would have been Natalie Cooper. "Poor poor dear, and now she is gone," Mrs. Messing whispered. She sobbed very hard, for the loss of Natalie as well as for the realization of what she had become.

Inside the church, Bishop Versey mournfully spoke to the heavens, "She was so full of radiant hope. There is no one who can fill her place in the world. With the death of Natalie Cooper, a lot of goodness has died. Lord, keep her with you."

He wept.

✳ ✳ ✳

Christelle followed her parents as they wandered aimlessly around the house. She comforted them as best as she could.

"Mama, Papa, Natalie is going to come back to us."

"What?" asked Mrs. Cooper.

"Natalie is going to come back to us," she told them.

"Why do you say that?" asked her mother.

"I don't know. I just feel it inside of me."

Bending down to meet her daughter face-to-face, Mrs. Cooper said softly, "Christelle, precious, Natalie has gone to heaven, and the only way that we are going to see her again is to get there ourselves."

"Mama, Natalie is coming home. You'll see!" she said matter-of-factly.

Mr. Cooper was quiet, secretly hoping that Christelle was right.

"What do you say, Papa?" Christelle asked.

Tears welled up in his eyes as he considered Christelle's faith. Then he answered with conviction, "I think that would be very fine—very fine indeed."

Leaving Christelle in her bedroom, Mr. Cooper escorted Mrs. Cooper to their adjacent room.

"She is no longer shedding tears," remarked Mrs. Cooper.

"No, Clarice, she's not."

"What do you think, Nathan? Is she just too young to understand, or do you think she knows something?"

"I wish I knew, Clarice. I am too numb to even venture a guess. Right or wrong, time will prove it out, that I know."

Mrs. Cooper walked into her husband's embrace. "Oh, Nathan, not again, not again! I can't bear losing Natalie. No one should have to bury a child, let alone two." Her shoulders shook with renewed sobs.

"You are quite right, my love. You are quite right." Mr. Cooper patted her back, feeling helpless. Soon his sobs blended with his wife's and they cried as one.

❄ ❄ ❄

Collin lay on his bed, exhausted from his second search with Constable Mallory, Mr. Cooper, and the others. He had shown them everything he had found, and nothing new had been learned. He wanted to be back out there, but the setting sun made it futile.

In Collin's despair he sat remembering Natalie. He always found her to be a great source of interest. Everything seemed to intrigue her, whether it was looking under rocks for bugs or learning some fascinating historical fact that he found boring. Her wit was quicker than his, which always kept him a little off balance. "Starting to freeze in places that have never before felt such cold!" he remembered her saying. "Indeed!"

Natalie could spend hours just looking at clouds, watching them change in both subtle and dramatic ways. She believed that if you could reach up and touch them you would find that they were the softest things imaginable. "Clouds are nature's poetry," she had said, "spoken at a whisper."

He had been bored after five minutes and found himself watching her instead. He remembered feeling clever after she caught him staring at her instead of watching clouds. "You are sunshine when the clouds block the light, Miss Cooper." With no idea where the words had come from, he had just said them, and the smile on her face showed her pleasure. Still she had made him go back to looking at some odd thing in the clouds that he could never quite see.

When he was looking at her it was easy to see depth in her eyes that as yet went unsounded. It was something that someday he had hoped to explore. He loved how her burnished-brown hair curled behind her pretty ears and fluffed whenever the wind decided to play with it. She was unaware that she was being longed for—that he wished he could just touch her hair with his face and kiss her cheek.

At school she was always helping the teachers, especially Mrs. Trubl, whom everyone loved. Natalie liked to help students who were having a hard time with anything that she herself understood. It was part of her nature.

Collin didn't know how she did it, but Natalie even managed to like Mrs. Messing. Natalie had said, "Some people are just sent to try us."

And then there was fishing. Collin's goal had been to one day catch either the biggest or the most fish—something he had yet to do. He was sure that he was the better fisherman, but Natalie always proved him otherwise. He lamented that he would not have more opportunities to assert his fishing prowess.

Memories and images of Natalie continued to invade Collin's attempt at sleep until exhaustion won out over his despair. That day all of Collin's dreams had died. His last thought before falling into the safety net of a dreamless sleep was that he immensely regretted not kissing Natalie when she had been in his arms a few days ago.

Earlier in the Same Day

The hunter had the turkey in his sights long enough to pull off the shot. Alerted, the bird moved just as the hunter fired, but it wasn't enough for a clean escape. Badly wounded, the big Tom took off at an incredible speed. The man discerned that it was headed for the Black River up ahead and a fishing hole that he was fond of. The last he saw of the bird, it was going over a rise. He very much wanted that turkey, so, leaving the sled behind, he began to chase it. Finding blood in the snow at the spot where the bird had been shot, his hope grew that he would not have to chase it very far.

As he came over the rise, he spied something to his left that turned out to be, of all things, a red bonnet partially hidden by the trunk of a tree. When he went to retrieve it, he saw both the turkey and a young girl. They appeared to be dead on the ice, just below him.

"What has happened here?" he wondered out loud.

The stunned hunter was shocked out of his confusion when a loud report suddenly cut through the air. The ice was crazing, cracking, and splitting underneath the prostrate body of the girl, and all at once she was gone, swept under the ice by the current. In a rush of panic that left his skin prickling, he flew into action. Dropping his gun he slid down the embankment and crashed onto the ice, his larger bulk breaking through in an instant. He had fished this part of the river often and knew it well. The water was only about three feet deep at most. He groped frantically for her under the edge of unbroken ice. He found her two feet away, pressed against a rock by the strong current. Feeling hair, he took hold and pulled her out and up. As he extracted her from the numbing cold she sputtered and coughed once, but was still deathly pale and unconscious. He shook her reflexively, trying to wake her up. With relief he noticed shallow breathing. "She's still alive!" he proclaimed to the stillness surrounding them. "But not for long," he added to himself. "To the cabin, or this will be the death of both of us."

Tired by the effort it had taken to save her, the hunter struggled to the edge of the river and laid the girl on her side. He left her briefly to retrieve the sled, hoping it would hold both the weight of his supplies and the girl. He guessed it would take nearly twenty minutes to get back to the cabin from the river and decided to dump the supplies. Time was critical. He would come back for them later.

Once he had the girl securely on the sled, it was slow going. It was snowing harder now and the wind was shrieking through the trees. Gusts whistled and roared in his ears, tearing at him, nipping him cruelly, and trying to rip his hands from the sled. He looked back at the girl and feared he would not be able to save her.

Because of the wind, the temperature was now a bitter, biting cold. The wet hunter was soon coated with frost. His cheeks and forehead were numb, and his fingers were starting to fail him. He wished he had taken off his gloves before charging into the river. With every step he took the sled became heavier, but he willed himself to keep going.

Though snow was piling thick on the girl, he could not take the time to brush her off. It was becoming nearly impossible to see. Squinting to lessen the wind on his face, he followed his own trail back to the cabin until the storm had obliterated all signs of it. Surrounding objects melted into one white nightmare, and he groped blindly through it. He slipped and fell, swallowing snow as he gasped for breath. He crawled back to his feet and took one purposeful step at a time—he hoped in the direction of the cabin. The cold had almost overtaken him, and now there was no more feeling in his extremities.

Were they close yet? Was he off track? With fading strength he wondered when their bodies would be found. At least whoever found them would know that he had tried to save the girl. Head down, and eyes closed for relief from the wind, he banged his head into a tree. Stunned out of his fog he saw that it was not a tree but the horizontal logs of his cabin. The door was only a few feet away!

With the last of his strength, the hunter kicked the door open and pulled the unconscious girl into his cabin, sled and all, before collapsing toward the fireplace. Feeling warmth on his face he opened his eyes to see the live embers of his banked fire. Sparked with new life, he crawled to the wood stacked next to the fireplace, and, with two clubs for hands, clumsily tossed on several small logs. With difficulty he removed his wet clothes, exposing his body to the warmth of the awakened flames. "For this relief, much thanks," he uttered, quoting Shakespeare.

"Now to help the girl." He felt for her pulse but couldn't find it. His hands were still too cold. She had a little breath of life, though it was ever so shallow. He went into action and gently rolled the girl out of the sled onto a cotton blanket. With thawing hands he proceeded to remove her melting clothing. In doing so he found a wound on the back of her head. It was not bleeding because of how cold she was, but it would need stitching.

What's this? Something was sticking out of her hair. He leaned forward to untangle it as carefully as his stiff fingers would allow. It was a feather—a turkey feather. *Why is a turkey feather . . . ?* A sick feeling filled the pit of his stomach as the scene of what had happened played in his mind. The turkey, flying blindly, had hit the girl from behind knocking her onto the ice. This tragedy had been caused by him, and he was the only one who could save her.

Placing her on the small bed he instinctively brushed the damp hair off her face and pulled the bed over near the fireplace. He covered her with his thinnest blanket so that most of the heat from the fire could penetrate to her skin. Frostbite would not be a problem, but pneumonia was a possibility. He wondered if she had swallowed any water during the short time she had been submerged. Now fully thawed himself, he dressed in dry clothes and put a pot of water over the fire.

Years as a doctor had taught Victor Ramsey to always be ready for the unexpected. Opening his bag, he selected his instruments, washed them and his hands in the hot water, and proceeded to tend to the girl's injury. The wetness of her hair made it easy to keep it off the wound while he stitched. She would be happy that her hair would hide the scar. After washing again and putting his instruments away, he gently laid her back on the pillow and took a good look at his patient for the first time. She had brown hair with a little natural curl. She might be quite striking but he couldn't be sure until her color improved. Blue-gray skin had never been conducive to beauty.

After some hours, Dr. Ramsey noted that she was passing through periods of hyperventilation and apnea. It had been several years since he had had a patient, but, being a naturally curious man, he had kept up on many developments in medicine after his retirement. He recalled that this type of breathing was called Cheyne-Stokes respiration, and it was one of the signs of coma. The young woman lying before him had indeed become comatose.

"Lord, I only have mortal hands. You're going to have to help me here." Suddenly he realized that it had been a great many years since he had asked for help from heaven. The last time was when his wife lay dying after childbirth. He watched the girl and sighed. "I don't have the heart to witness another death, so I'll just have to pull her through," he decided with resolve.

Dr. Ramsey recalled that the few patients who had come to him in a coma had different outcomes—combinations of physical, intellectual, and psychological difficulties. They often had posttraumatic amnesia, where recovery of memory was dependant on how long the patient had been in a coma. All had needed close, long-term attention. He knew that many days might go by before there was any improvement. The most common cause of death for a person in a coma was a secondary infection, such as pneumonia, especially for those who lay still for extended periods of time. In an effort to prevent this type of complication, he decided to move the girl into different positions several times each day.

He examined her for "doll's eyes" by lifting her eyelids one at a time and moving her head from side to side. With relief he saw that her eyes moved opposite the direction of the turning of her head; however, coma was reaffirmed when he noted the dilation of both pupils.

For the remainder of the first day Dr. Ramsey busied himself by attending to his patient and his supplies. In between these tasks he did a little reading and watched the weather. While caring for the girl's clothes, he came upon a little clump of mistletoe within the inside pocket of her coat and wondered who it was from—or who it was for. He laid the mistletoe on the fireplace mantel and hung her washed clothes around the cabin to dry. He was grateful that nothing required repair. "I can sew up people very neatly, but my needle-and-thread skills for clothing leave something to be desired," he mused. A hired seamstress always saved him the trouble when his own clothes needed attention.

The terrible snow squall had stopped soon after he had miraculously found the cabin. Looking out his only window, he could see a faint glow in spaces between the clouds. The sun was trying to burn its way through. He hoped the sun would win.

He turned away from the window and walked to the table, considering what else he could do. His eyes came to rest on a small pile of paper he kept on hand for correspondence, and that gave him an idea. He would keep a record of her care. Not only would it help pass the time, but it would most likely be useful since his memory wasn't quite what it used to be.

December 12, 1881
At the Cabin

Early the next morning after attending to the girl, Dr. Ramsey made a dash for the supplies he had left behind. After loading them onto his sleigh, he found the turkey—a snow-covered lump on the ice—now nicely frozen. Retrieving it would depend on whether or not the ice would hold his weight today. Unfortunately it was just barely out of reach from the shore, so he would have to chance going onto the ice.

Gingerly he inched out, listening intently for any sign of breaking. At the first sign of failure he would abandon the idea. Fortunately he was able to creep close enough to get a grip on the turkey and pull it off the ice without incident.

Not wanting to be away from the girl any longer, he added the prize to his load and headed back, all the while scanning the sky for menacing weather.

He hurried into the cabin to check on his patient. She was still unresponsive and hadn't moved. He took a moment to turn her onto her right side, hoping to thwart pneumonia.

Later he went back out to check on his team of horses to see if they were all right. He found them both in good spirits. He was sorry that he wasn't going to be able to take them out for a while.

In Town

Collin, fidgeting as though he were sleeping on thorns, jerked his elbows and sat up. He did not know where he was or why he was there. Then it all came flooding back. His nightmare was not a nightmare. The events of yesterday had actually happened, and Natalie was gone. He was still exhausted. It took all his strength to get out of bed, and all he could think of was finding her. He dressed and went to find his father.

"Pa, I'm going back out to look for Natalie's body."

"I hope you find her, son. It's going to be tough going with all the ice on the river."

"I know, but I have to try."

"I understand," replied Mr. Bradley. "She sure was a sweet thing."

"Much more than that, Pa."

"Yes, much, much more, Collin! It's a shame that she had to go and get herself drowned, all on account of mistletoe," He said shaking his head in pity. "You take as long as you like. We can manage without you, even for a few days."

"Thanks. I'll be back before dark, Pa."

"Good luck, son." As Mr. Bradley watched Collin leave, he thought, "That mistletoe should have been for you, boy."

December 13, 1881
At the Cabin

On the third day Dr. Ramsey's patient started drifting in and out of consciousness. Though her color was more normal, she was not fully back in the world of the living. More often than not his attempts at getting her to drink something resulted in having to take care of the spillage. He couldn't tell if she actually drank anything at all. However, her breathing sounded clear, which was a good sign that pneumonia was staying away.

In between taking care of the girl, he spent time looking out the window. He decided that if any turkeys should come by the cabin, which they often did, he would make every effort to get another. He and the girl might be there a while. To increase his chances he had his shotgun loaded and propped up by the door.

While time moved slowly, he continued to attend to his notes and his reading and to watch for improvement.

December 14, 1881
At the Cabin

On the fourth day the girl awoke for a few moments in a profound state of confusion. His attempts at giving her water proved more fruitful this time. It was obvious that she couldn't see him because her eyes never focused on anything. He hoped the blow to the back of her head had not caused permanent blindness. His attempts to get her to respond to his questions were futile, and soon she was again in a deep sleep.

Dr. Ramsey didn't see any turkeys, but the weather was still clear. If by chance she recovered quickly, he could get her home before another snow came. Spying the mistletoe on the mantle, he wondered again about it. Had it been given to her as a gift, or was it waiting to be used for someone special? Either way, the young man was very lucky. Now that she had her color back, he could see that she was quite pretty.

In Town

Waking to a new day in his living nightmare, Collin emerged from his bed feeling the numbness of his loss. Deep hurt had settled in, and he was always on the verge of tears.

"Natalie, Natalie, where are you?" he whispered to himself.

He desperately wanted to find her so that her parents would have more than just memories to bury. For the past two days he had searched for several miles downstream with diminishing hope. He knew it was likely that her body was stuck somewhere under the ice, probably not far from where she had drowned. Today he would go back to the hole in the ice and start looking again.

December 15, 1881
At the Cabin

Dr. Ramsey woke up to see that it was snowing heavily. He turned to his patient. "Well, I guess we're staying here a while."

He observed the girl carefully and with curiosity. Whatever nightmares she had been having, they were not in evidence today. Her sleep was more peaceful. Her lungs remained clear, and his fears about pneumonia were lessening. He still had no answers about the possibility of blindness. Come what may, she was in God's hands. He paused. That was the second time that he had remembered God. He resolved to remain bitter.

Along the Black River

Collin trudged along the river fighting the snow and stopping at all the open water where swift currents wouldn't let it ice over. He stared intently through the whiteness for some sign of Natalie, willing her to appear. He knew now that he loved her more than life itself—something she would never know. He loathed himself for not telling her, and now it was forever too late. Today was his last chance to find her before the funeral. He had failed her parents and he had failed himself. He began to think that he should just jump into the freezing river and join Natalie under the ice. It would be so easy. If he chose the right spot, the swift current would quickly carry him under. There would be no rethinking, no saving himself, no going back to the pain of living without her.

December 16, 1881
At the Cabin

Natalie's first impression upon coming out of her fog was that she was not at home. It smelled different—wood-like, with a hint of smoke. Her vision was blurry, as though she were looking through thin ice. She knew that someone was near, but she couldn't quite make out where. Her head also ached terribly, and she was thirsty and felt like she could eat a horse.

"Hello?" she asked timidly.

"Ah, good! You're awake! How do you feel?" said a man's voice.

"Terrible!"

"Please, could you describe your symptoms?"

"Symptoms?"

"Yes. I'm Dr. Ramsey. I found you and brought you to my cabin. Now, tell me about how you're feeling, and then you can tell me who you are.

"I have a dreadful headache, and my vision is very fuzzy. I can't quite see you. And I'm thirsty and hungry. Oh, and I'm Natalie Cooper."

"Headache and fuzzy vision, not so good; thirst and hunger, very good. Natalie Cooper, I'm pleased to make your acquaintance. You struck your head, and the blow was hard enough to cause a concussion. With a little more time, your vision should clear," he added encouragingly, though he wasn't so sure himself. "Also, when you fell you received a cut to the back of your head, which I sewed up for you. That was five days ago. A couple more days and the stitches can come out. The very best news is that you have not had a fever and did not come down with pneumonia."

Natalie felt for the wound and winced. It was tender to the touch. "Can I get some water, please?"

"Oh yes, certainly. Here," he said, putting a small cup to her mouth. "I had a very difficult time with my efforts to get you to drink. No, no, don't sit up. You're not dressed."

Natalie had just enough time to catch her covers. "Have I been in this state of undress the whole time?"

"Yes, of course. It was the best way to take care of you and attend to your needs. I have your clothes here all tidied up. You may dress whenever you feel like you can do it yourself. I will continue to help you with anything you require. I am your doctor, and you are my first patient since I retired in . . . let's see . . . three years."

Natalie didn't know how to feel. She had never in her whole life been in the presence of a man with no clothes on, doctor or not.

"Where is this place?" she asked, changing the subject.

Dr. Ramsey replied, "It is very near the Black River, maybe four miles from Chester."

"That means we might be near the Cooper Mill."

"Oh yes, it's just over the hill. Maybe two miles or so as the crow flies. Easy walking in good weather; nearly impossible with all the snow coming down."

"How long are we going to be here?" she asked.

"A few more days, I think. I won't risk your health until you are well enough to travel, which you most certainly are not."

She calculated quickly. *I fell on December eleventh and I've been here five days. This must be the sixteenth.* "So today is the sixteenth of December?" she inquired out loud.

"Yes."

"Do you think I will be home for Christmas?" she asked anxiously.

"I can't say. I do hope so. Your family needs to know that you are all right."

"They must think I'm dead—and for five days! This is terrible, just terrible. We need to get word to them that I'm alive!" she exclaimed.

"Yes, quite likely, and no, simply not possible. You are still in too much danger to travel, and I won't risk leaving you here by yourself because I don't know exactly how long it would take me to get word to your family. Also, getting back could prove difficult if the weather changes as suddenly as it did before. We both nearly died when a very severe snowstorm overtook us while I was trying to get you here. This knot on the top of my head is proof of my sacrifice for you," he said, touching the still-tender spot. Seeing the disappointment register on her face, he tried to reassure her. "I promise that I will take you home at the very first opportunity."

Feeling bereaved and knowing that nothing could be done about it, Natalie lay back down and had a good cry.

In Town

Natalie would have been very pleased with how the church has been decorated for Christmas this year, thought Bishop

Versey. He looked out over the audience of mourners. His gaze stopped for a moment on the candlesticks that had magically appeared. Today they were aglow with the light from new, tall white candles. He was almost certain it was Natalie who had brought them, but how she knew that one had been broken was still a mystery.

Bishop Versey couldn't remember the last time the chapel was so full, especially for the funeral of such a young person. Usually funerals of this size were for someone who had lived a long and fruitful life and had known a lot of people. He recognized that he had come to love the girl, and those in attendance were a testament to all the lives she had touched. Bishop Versey felt prepared to give Natalie a proper eulogy but was unsure if he would be able to get through the service without being overcome with emotion.

Mr. and Mrs. Cooper and Christelle were seated up front, and off to his right sat Mrs. Adams and her son. The Bradleys were nowhere to be seen. The bishop had just learned that Collin had been quite fond of Natalie, which gave him cause to wonder where they were. Bishop Versey stood up and quietly cleared his throat. The words came out just loud enough to get everyone's attention.

"Brothers and sisters, we are gathered here to remember Miss Natalie Catherine Cooper. Miss Cooper loved everyone, and by the looks of it—with how many of us are here—everyone loved her. I know I did. It is so very difficult when we lose a young person, especially one as choice as Miss Cooper, before they have had a chance to fulfill a complete measure of life. I submit to you that Natalie in her nearly seventeen years had a more fulfilling life than most because, as far as I could see, she lived the Lord's gospel every day. She was always about Christ's business. Since her passing, many have told me stories of how she touched their lives. Most of these incidents I was completely unaware of. . . ."

December 17, 1881
At the Cabin

Natalie's vision began clearing, and she was able to focus on her surroundings inside the cabin. It was a very small structure, maybe twenty feet to each side. The dominant feature in the cabin was the fireplace. It had been set up for simple cooking, with a large kettle hook in the center. Natalie smiled. The mantle held her precious mistletoe, as well as a metal pitcher and two small cooking pots. To the right hung large forks and tongs for handling large game, possibly deer. On the left there was a good-sized pile of wood—enough for several more days, she guessed.

The cabin was furnished with a sturdy table, a small writing desk, and a chair. Natalie was on the smaller of two beds, and she could see that they had been made by the same hands. She was certain hers had been created for a little girl because it had brightly painted posts, and she could just make out the remains of painted flowers. She also noticed that her bed was designed to slide under the larger of the two to save space.

The cabin was well maintained, but it looked as though it had been used for many years. She wondered if this might be the cabin that she and Collin had once found during one of their childhood outings. It seemed about the right size. *It must be,* she decided.

Dr. Ramsey looked to be in his late sixties. He was nearly as tall as her father, and they had the same color of eyes. He had wavy snow-white hair that was combed back and a beard to match. He looked to be very fit. He must be, since he was strong enough to save her, for which she was eternally grateful.

"Dr. Ramsey, may I ask you a question?"

"Yes, Miss Cooper, what is it?"

"I don't recall ever seeing you in Chester."

"I'm not from around here. I make my home in Bayonne, which is forty-five miles away by train. I bought this cabin last year so that I would have a place to stay while I hunt. This cabin used to belong to an acquaintance of mine."

"Do you come here often?"

"I do now that I am retired."

"Thank you. I was confused as to why I had never seen you before, since you live so close to Chester."

"I hope to become more acquainted with Chester. Maybe you can help me to make introductions."

"I would be happy to," replied Natalie.

"Thank you, Miss Cooper."

Natalie was grateful that her vision had improved. She spent the rest of the day watching the smoke and flames in the fireplace make an endless variety of interesting forms. Most lasted but a moment and then slipped away, forever gone, preserved only in her memories. It was funny how entertaining a fire could be when there was simply nothing else to do.

In Town

Collin lay in bed loathing himself more than ever. He had not found Natalie, and now he had missed her funeral.

"I'm sorry that we couldn't let you go to the funeral," said Mrs. Bradley, as she came into Collin's room carrying a cup of tea. "Your father and I love you and have no interest in attending *your* funeral. All of your searching has exhausted you. You did the best you could in your searches for Miss Cooper—more than anyone. I'm very proud of you. I will send your father to see the bishop and learn about how it went." She kissed Collin on the side of his forehead and was dismayed to discover fever.

December 20, 1881
At the Cabin

Natalie went to the window to survey the cold December scene. All the snow from a nor'easter dimmed her hope of getting home by Christmas. Everything in sight was white and covered with three feet of snow. There was no going out in that. They were snowbound. It would be all that Dr. Ramsey could do to feed and care for his horses. She steeled herself for the stay in order to push away the worry that she might miss Christmas at home. Natalie turned from the window, vexed as to what she could do to bring a little Christmas to this sparse, cramped little cabin.

Dr. Ramsey sat writing at his desk, working on his patient report about Natalie. He had the satisfaction of knowing that she was going to be all right, and it was going to be a lot of fun returning her to her family. This would be the first time in his career that he had brought someone back from the dead.

"Dr. Ramsey, could I trouble you for a piece of paper?"

"Of course. Just one?" he asked.

"Yes, one will do."

He handed her the sheet of paper, finished his notes, and then brought out a book and began to read. Natalie sat down and considered what to make. After some moments she decided to make a Star of Bethlehem, as her mother called it, because that is what her father called his special ornament. Her mother had taught her how to fold them when she was a little girl, and she had made many, but not for some years. She started to fold the paper with the mountain and valley folds that she had been taught, and it was not long before she was finished.

Natalie admired her handiwork. Christmas was coming, and she was going to miss it, but she could put up some Christmas in the cabin, even if it was only one little decoration. Looking up she considered where to put the star, and the answer was obvious: centered up over the fireplace.

Sensing motion, Dr. Ramsey glanced up from reading and saw Natalie holding an eight-pointed star. He closed his eyes. Seeing it stirred distant memories—memories that he wanted to forget, memories that he had worked hard to push away because of the pain they caused. However, not wanting to disappoint Natalie, he took a deep breath and drove the memories back again. Looking to her he asked, "What are you going to do with that?"

"Put it up over the fireplace mantle, if I can figure out how to attach it," she replied with satisfaction.

"I think I can help with that," he said. Rising from his chair, he walked over to his bag, produced a piece of string, and handed it to her. "You can hang it from the center rafter."

She could see that the wooden beam he was pointing out traversed the length of the cabin and ended directly over the fireplace. "Wonderful!" she responded joyfully. Whereupon she moved her chair toward the fireplace, stood up on it, and reached for the beam. Too short! She tried standing on tiptoe. Still too short.

"Here, let me do that," Dr. Ramsey offered.

They exchanged places. His reach was just high enough to get the string up and over the beam. He tied it so that the string dangled above the center of the mantle. "That should do nicely," he said. "Now you can attach your star."

Natalie considered for a moment and decided that since there was no paste to be had, it would be necessary to put a hole in the star. She set it on the table and used the cooking knife to pierce the ornament. With anticipation she bounced up onto the chair as light as a feather and hung the decoration. Then she jumped down and admired their work.

Natalie turned to face Dr. Ramsey. "Oh thank you!" she told him, her eyes bright with joy.

The depth of Natalie's gratitude touched Dr. Ramsey. "You are quite welcome," he replied.

"I just had to have some Christmas in here. This will have to do."

"I don't have Christmas in my heart anymore," Dr. Ramsey revealed. "I haven't celebrated it for some thirty-eight years, and I don't propose to start now. But I am happy to let you have your Christmas, however small it is. Losing my wife and son took it out of me."

"Well, I think we're just going to have to put it back in there," she replied, tapping a spot over his heart with her delicate hand.

Dr. Ramsey looked past Natalie, absorbed with memories of his wife. He had never told anyone his story, and he found himself very much wanting to share it with this girl who had so dramatically entered his life. He looked to see if he had Natalie's attention. She had seated herself at the table and was gazing at him with encouragement. He moved his chair so that he sat directly across from her and began.

"After I married Evie, I decided to take her to America. I had money, and I wanted to get her away from my overbearing father. I knew that if we stayed in England, he would try to control her just like he tried to control everyone else. We might have stayed if my mother had remained alive. She was very skilled at softening the blows of my father. That was how I survived growing up. My mother was the buffer between us. But she was gone, and it was my desire to get far away from the source of my hate. My only regret was that I would miss my sister.

"It was on the ship to New York that I first began to feel that I might actually become my own person. I had feared becoming my father and had chosen to be a doctor to ensure that if my father ever cut me off, which was often threatened, I could make it on my own. Marrying Evie and leaving England were two of the best decisions I ever made.

"Your star reminds me of a little incident that took place on the ship during our crossing to America. I met a man who was returning from the city of Sonneberg, Germany, which he said was very well known for toy making, if I recall correctly. As time passed on the ship, Evie and I had the opportunity to get to know him. He was quite genial and we liked him.

"One day, just before docking in New York, he came to me while I was alone. He produced a small wooden box that was about twelve inches on each side, maybe a little more. When he opened it I saw the most beautiful Christmas ornaments I had ever seen—four of them, each a little different from the others. He said that they were the first of their kind, and that no one had ever been able to produce glass ornaments like them before, especially that large. He was taking them home to try and secure orders for the coming Christmas season.

"He revealed that he had been foolish and gambled too much money on the crossing and was now short of funds to make it all the way home. He had no other option but to sell one of his ornaments. At that moment I decided that I should have one for Evie. I asked him how much he was short. Just now I recall his name: It was Coleman. I decided to give Mr. Coleman the amount he needed, and I chose an eight-pointed silver star. He was grateful, and I was happy that I had procured this beautiful little ornament for my first Christmas with Evie.

"I presented it to her on Christmas Eve. She was delighted with the gift and said that she would treasure it for the rest of her life. And she did." His voice trailed off, and he took a moment to compose himself.

"She died the following year just after I delivered our baby," he continued. "I had never been a man who was accustomed to crying, but after I lost Evie, my whole body seemed to grieve—no, not just my body, my whole soul. I just wept on and on to the point of exhaustion."

Dr. Ramsey stopped abruptly as these memories became too painful to be relived. "Enough of that," he said with such force that Natalie decided not to press him for more.

By noon the skies had cleared and it became warmer outside. The snow began to thaw. The change in the air made its way into the cabin, and Natalie felt it.

In Town

Collin's fever and pain from losing Natalie kept his mind in a state of darkness. He had no energy or desire to leave the house—or his room for that matter. He no longer cared that Christmas was coming. He was entirely absorbed in contemplation of her and what might have been. All he could do was stare at his most prized possession: her red bonnet, hung carefully on the hat rack in his room.

December 21, 1881
At the Cabin

Natalie first sensed that her toes were cold. She pulled them back under the warmth of the covers and poked out a hand to test the air. Cold. Pulling the covers off her face she sat up quickly to find that the fire was nearly out and that Dr. Ramsey had not yet risen. Ever since they had been thrown together by fate, he was always the first one up. Why not today?

Gingerly she coaxed her feet to the cold floor and quickly trotted to the woodpile. After bringing the fire back to life, she glanced around and discovered that Dr. Ramsey was still in bed—a big lump of blankets with his back to her.

As she contemplated the situation, she noticed that he appeared to be shaking. Quietly she went over to take a closer look. Hovering very near to him, she listened, and what she heard made her heart race. He was shivering hard. He was sick. A surge of worry gripped her: He was her only way back home. Even more, how was she to care for a sick man? Her mother had always taken care of the family when they were sick, and Natalie had never seen her father sick. What was she to do?

Natalie remembered seeing her mother take care of Christelle once when Christelle was very small. Her mother had been very concerned about fever, saying that fever was a killer—or could be.

How did one check for fever? Dr. Ramsey suddenly rolled onto his back, exposing his face to her. He was covered in sweat. Finding a cloth, she wiped off his forehead and face. As she touched his face she felt heat. His forehead felt even hotter. It must be fever. Why had she not concerned herself more with medicine and knowing what to do in situations like this? The answer to that question was simple: her mother had always intervened and had made her stay away from anyone who became sick. Benjamin had fallen ill by catching a sickness from someone else, and her brother had died. Her mother didn't want the same thing to happen to Natalie.

Natalie went to the doctor's bag to see what she might learn. It would be nice to find a set of instructions. What she discovered was almost as good. She found his notes about how he had been taking care of her, and he had made a note of how he might treat her if he needed to drop a fever quickly: He thought he might use clean snow.

Moments later Dr. Ramsey returned to the world of consciousness.

"Dr. Ramsey, what's wrong?" exclaimed Natalie.

"I have 'rich man's disease,'" he said with a shaky voice.

"What?" she asked, thinking that she hadn't heard him correctly.

"I have 'rich man's disease,' also known as gout. It often attacks me after I've been chilled. I think that little dip in the river might have done it to me this time. It bit me early this morning," he rasped. "It started with pain in my feet, specifically my big toes—which are now on fire, I might add.

Then the chills and shivers set in and this time a fever. I've been suffering the torture of this condition off and on over the years. It usually goes away in about a week."

"A week!" exclaimed Natalie. "That's past Christmas."

"I'm afraid so," he said with sympathy. He groaned and shifted his position in the bed.

"I know you're anxious to get home, but with this attack of gout being in my feet, I can't walk. I'm also too tired and weak to get up just yet. You'll have to be my nurse and take care of me just as I took care of you, and you will have to attend to the horses. I am sorry to have to put you through this, my dear girl."

❄ ❄ ❄

Natalie's night passed in tortured sleeplessness. She was kept awake by Dr. Ramsey's tossing and turning at all hours in his effort to get comfortable despite his incessant pain. Her anguish at not being able to tell her family that she was alive and well also kept sleep at bay. And she worried about Collin, the weather, and how much longer it would take for the snow to melt so they could use the sleigh. She also feared that Dr. Ramsey would not get well this time. She cried several times throughout the night and into the next morning.

December 22, 1881
At the Cabin

Just before dawn Natalie had a thought: If snow worked to reduce a fever, which is heat, then why wouldn't the snow help to reduce the fire in Dr. Ramsey's toes? She would try the snow for his fever and his feet, just as soon as she could get things ready.

Dr. Ramsey awakened to find Natalie putting snow on the floor next to his bed. "What are you doing, Miss Cooper?"

"Dr. Ramsey, I have an idea that might help lessen the pain. Please sit up and slide your feet off the bed."

As Dr. Ramsey's feet felt the cold they recoiled, but the momentary relief from the fire in his big toes made him put them back. When he saw what Natalie had done he thought it quite ingenious. She had used four logs from the woodpile to make a rectangle large enough to accommodate his feet, and then she had filled the rectangle with snow. He was in between the tortures of cold and pain and had to make a decision. The cold was reducing the pain in his feet, so he chose to bear the cold of the snow over the pain of the gout. His feet, once numbed, were happier. Next Natalie attacked his fever with a little snow sandwiched between layers of cloth.

"It looks like you have found the solution for relieving the pain in my toes. I think the snow is going to help my fever also. Let's keep giving both a try, shall we?" said Dr. Ramsey.

"Yes I think we should," she agreed. "I remember that when I crossed the Atlantic from France, they put my feet in ice water for my seasickness, I found no relief, but I am grateful that this is working for you."

At the Cooper Home

Mrs. Cooper sat motionless in her blue rocking chair with her hands in her lap. She was staring off past the poinsettia that Natalie had given to her as an early Christmas present. She was in no mood to move or even get dressed, but soon Christelle would be up and would need her attention.

Mr. Cooper had kissed her good morning some hours ago and then had slipped out to do the chores that Natalie used to do, as well as his own.

Mrs. Cooper felt welded to the chair. After the loss of Benjamin, her grief was always just under her skin, but she had learned over the years how to keep it pushed away. With the death of Natalie it had resurfaced, and she was having a terrible time getting control of it. Two children—she had lost two children—and Christelle, bless her for a long life, was all that she had left. She wanted to protect her and keep her shielded from harm, but she knew that that would not be good for her. She would have to keep doing what she had always done for Christelle and not become overprotective. But that was not what her heart wanted to do.

As she focused on the poinsettia, she sat thinking that this beautiful red flower was the only living thing that linked her to her daughter. She was going to make it live forever. She got up and walked stiffly over to the flowering plant and picked it up. "I am now connected to you because you are connected to my Natalie," she said out loud. She felt the red petals soft on her cheek and then kissed them. As she sat it down she pressed a cold finger into the soil of the pot. She should water it and go see to Christelle.

December 23, 1881
In the Cabin

The snow was melting, Natalie found herself brooding about missing Christmas at home. Dr. Ramsey still needed her, even though his feet were starting to improve.

Her dark mood was interrupted by Dr. Ramsey. "If you wish, I'll tell you about the first Christmas that I never celebrated, and then you might understand why I don't like Christmas."

Dr. Ramsey's words snapped her back to the present. She looked directly at him without saying anything. She was trying to decide if she wanted to hear about it, though it would be a better distraction than what she had been doing. She nodded to show her interest, adding a little smile.

"After the birth of our baby, Evie lingered unconscious for a few days. Mrs. Copper, the wet nurse, cared for the baby while I cared for Evie. But even with all my medical training I was not able to save her. She died late in the evening on Christmas Day. I never got to speak to her after the baby came—not even to say goodbye. I watched her as carefully as I could, looking for any little sign of improvement, and when none came and the outcome was assured, I could only wait. As her time neared to cross over, I made a futile attempt to rouse her to say goodbye. I only wanted a moment, and it was denied me. My last act was to kiss her just after she had taken her last breath."

With a heavy sigh of regret Dr. Ramsey continued. "My world shattered. For selfish reasons, I felt no attachment to the baby, so I arranged for Mrs. Copper to take him to England to be cared for by my sister. But my sister never received the child, and I never saw him again."

Dr. Ramsey looked as though he had fallen into a daze. The luster in his eyes darkened, and Natalie could see that he was no longer with her.

"Mrs. . . . . Copper, Mrs. Copper," he growled. "Mrs. Copper. . . . That woman stole my son."

Dr. Ramsey blinked and met Natalie's eyes. "She must have, having just recently lost her own child. I became convinced that the theft of my baby was a direct punishment from God for rejecting the child." Dr. Ramsey sighed and turned his gaze to the fireplace, saying nothing more.

Natalie, not knowing what to say, also said nothing.

December 24, 1881
In the Cabin

Natalie was very pleased with how the turkey was coming along. She had never cooked one by herself. Her mother had always done it, and the thought had never occurred to her to learn. But as far as she was concerned, it was just a big chicken, and she had cooked dozens of those. However, handling the big bird proved intimidating, especially with all the feathers and not having an oven. Her arms ached from turning it on the spit over the fire. She had decided to cook it with its skin on as a barrier against the flames.

Once the turkey was done to her satisfaction, she peeled off the black skin, and they dug into the layers below.

The bird was a little dry but tasted good. *Thank the heavens for salt,* she thought, *which makes everything taste better.*

Natalie was thoughtful during dinner, and when they were finished eating, she asked a question that had been on her mind. "Dr. Ramsey, I have never been able to figure out how I ended up in the river."

"That, my dear girl, you could say was my fault. But you can be comforted knowing that you have had a little revenge."

"I haven't had any revenge on you, Dr. Ramsey. Besides, no matter what you did I would never seek revenge."

"The culprit was that turkey," he said pointing to the remains. "When I wounded the bird, he took off flying blind at great speed. He collided with you from behind and knocked you onto the frozen river. I arrived only moments later to see both you and that turkey looking very dead on the ice. I can tell you I was really stunned at what I saw before me. I didn't have a clue as to how it had happened. When the ice broke up beneath you, I had no time to consider it. It was only after I found a turkey feather in your hair that I was able to put the mystery together."

"You mean to tell me that I was almost done in by a turkey?" she asked, smiling.

"Yes, and now by eating the culprit you have had a little retribution."

"Hit by a turkey—that would have to be a first, I should think."

"I would quite agree," He said. "Now I have a question for you—about that mistletoe that I discovered in your coat."

Natalie blushed. "I had just picked it when I was struck by your turkey. I had hoped to use it for Collin Bradley, a boy that I am very fond of. I know it makes me seem very forward, but I love him," she said longingly.

"He's a very lucky fellow."

"Thank you, Dr. Ramsey." Changing the subject Natalie asked, "Dr. Ramsey, what color was the ornament that you gave your wife? I can't recall it."

"Silver," he said without thinking. Then he paused and continued, "No . . . no, it wasn't just silver. It was silver with pairs of blue, gold, and red rays. I don't know how I could have forgotten that. It was very beautiful."

"And where is that ornament now?"

"Why? What a strange question."

"I'm sorry. I was just thinking that I should like to see it if you still had it."

"No, I no longer have it in my possession. With no more Christmases with Evie, it was just too painful to keep. I gave it to Mrs. Copper as a parting gift, along with—I might add— quite a bit of money to ensure that she should have no trouble getting back to England. I sent a letter with her addressed to my sister, Mrs. Spencer. It instructed my bank that my sister should be given whatever funds were required, within reason, to see to the welfare of the baby. Mrs. Copper must have posed as my sister and used the money for herself."

"Are you sure the child made it to England?"

"No, I'm not. I did, however, put them both on the ship with instructions to the captain that they should be well attended to. After that I don't know what happened to them. Anything, I suppose! I regret sending the child away more than anything else I have ever done."

"I'm sorry," Natalie said sympathetically.

Dr. Ramsey slipped his sore feet into his sheepskin slippers. *My! What comfort,* he thought, *just to be able to walk again.* He got up out of his chair, gingerly stepped over to the window, and looked at the rapidly melting snow. "We might get out of here tomorrow—just in time for your Christmas."

"We have an appointment with the living then?" chirped Natalie with excitement.

"Yes, I think so," replied Dr. Ramsey. "If the sleigh is not stuck too tight, I think it will be safe to go."

The news was almost too good to be true. With rapidly rising spirits, Natalie allowed herself to imagine the joyful reunion with her family and friends, and Collin most of all.

December 25, 1881
In the Cabin

Christmas morning was bathed in a soft apricot glow. The stillness of the trees was interrupted only by the quiet passing of small birds on their way to find winter morsels.

Dr. Ramsey readied his team; the manes of the mares were covered in a silvery frost. They breathed on their master's hands as he fed them and told them about his expectations of the coming morning. Though not interested in Christmas for himself, he felt great excitement and anticipation for what lay ahead. To take Natalie home and present her to her parents—what joy!

"Miss Cooper!"

Natalie emerged from the cabin looking radiant. Dr. Ramsey helped her up and into the sleigh and carefully tucked a coverlet around her.

"Will this be enough?" he asked.

"Yes, thank you," she replied as she settled in cozily.

"Do you have your mistletoe?"

Looking up, she nodded. Her gaze met Dr. Ramsey's, and she saw the truth of something she had suspected about him confirmed in his eyes. *This will be the best Christmas ever,* she thought.

Natalie took a deep breath. She was in the midst of a morning of marvelous expectations. She wanted to remember exactly what this particular Christmas morning felt like. She closed her eyes, and with a little tilt of her head, sunshine poured like warm liquid onto her upturned face. With a little "giddy-up" from Dr. Ramsey they were off, and she was finally on her way home.

At the Cooper Home

Christmas morning arrived at the Cooper household the same way it had for the last couple of years: Christelle bounced into Mr. and Mrs. Cooper's bedroom and up onto the bed. "It's Christmas!" she sang to her sleeping parents. Not getting the response she desired, she bounced again and landed on her hands and knees right between them. Seeing them stir, she let out another yell: "It's Christmas!"

In spite of how they felt inside, Mr. and Mrs. Cooper had decided they were going to show Christelle a happy Christmas and make it the best that they could. One thing was sure: they were too heartbroken to go to the day's church services.

They made merry for Christelle. When her father said that she could have Natalie's Christmas stocking, Christelle was adamant that it should not be disturbed. Deciding not to upset her, he said that they would wait until later.

Mr. Cooper quietly read the letter to Natalie from the Savior that Mrs. Cooper had written Christmas Eve. Mrs. Cooper had told him that writing it was the only way that she was going to get through Christmas Day.

With some apprehension, he read:

Dear Natalie,

I am very happy to have you back with me. It has been a joy to see you stay true when so many others stray from the path that was set for them. I hope that your homecoming has been a happy one. You now know of the love felt by all on this side of immortality and that in the blink of an eye your family will be with you.

Tear stains interrupted the letter. Then came the rest—this time from Mrs. Cooper's heart.

Natalie, I miss you terribly. I know that you are now with Benjamin, and for that I am grateful. He has his little sister that he loved so much back with him. He is going to be in for quite a shock, for you have grown into such a lovely young woman. I am going to miss deeply the happiness that you brought to us simply by being you. I am going to grieve that Christelle is not going to have you around for the wonderful example that you were. But most of all I am going to miss being able to see you marry and watching you experience the joy of having your own family. Bishop Versey said that you had filled the full measure of your life, and I believe that he was right. I only wish that you hadn't done it so soon. I miss you and Benjamin so much that I can hardly go on, but I know that I must be strong for Christelle and your papa, and I will. Until we meet again.

Love to you from me, your mama, always and forever.

The knot in Mr. Cooper's throat had become tight. He shared his wife's sentiments, and missed Natalie and Benjamin terribly. After wiping away his tears, he carefully folded up the letter and tucked it into his vest pocket.

Mr. Cooper's thoughts were interrupted by the beautiful sound of sleigh bells. No one was expected. Maybe someone had only just heard about Natalie and was coming to pay their respects. He didn't have the heart for visitors, but whoever it was, he would receive them.

Peering through the window he could make out a sleigh with two passengers—one large and one small—but the glass was too frosted to make out any other details. He would just have to wait.

Mr. Cooper started toward the door, forced a smile, and was stunned as the smaller of the two burst through the door without even the slightest knock. "Mama! Papa! Christelle! I'm home!" she called.

Natalie flew into him, throwing her arms around him. The moments of bewilderment passed quickly. His daughter had returned from the dead, or so it seemed! Christelle had said that she would come home, and there she was—not as a ghost but in the flesh. Mrs. Cooper cried, "Natalie!" and ran forward with Christelle following close behind.

Christelle took her mother by the hand, yanking it over and over again to get her attention. Looking up into her mother's shocked face, she said, "I told you, Mama. I told you Natalie would come back."

Secure in her father's embrace, Natalie gazed up at him and said, "Papa, I'm all right."

Mrs. Cooper, doubting her eyes and ears, stole Natalie from her husband and held her as tightly as she could, experiencing the greatest joy of her life.

"My darling child," cried Mrs. Cooper, "you have come back to me!" Then she proceeded to cover her face with kisses and happy tears.

"Yes, Mama, I have, and I'm all right. . . . I'm all right now that I am home with you."

Mr. Cooper turned to the unknown man and asked, "How can I ever thank you?"

Dr. Ramsey stood just inside the door, not wanting to intrude on the heartwarming reunion. "There is no need, Mr. Cooper. You have a very lovely daughter. It was a pleasure taking care of her. She in turn took care of me when my gout flared up, for which I am eternally grateful."

Christelle, tugging on Dr. Ramsey's coat asked the white-bearded man, "Are you Santa Clause?"

"He is today!" declared Natalie.

Parting from her mother's embrace, she swept Christelle up into her arms and planted great big kisses on both cheeks. A moment later she introduced Dr. Ramsey and explained to her mother and father the details of her two-week absence.

When she finished her story, Natalie turned to Dr. Ramsey with a mischievous twinkle in her eyes. "You don't know how happy I am to have a grandfather."

Perplexed, Dr. Ramsey let the comment pass, deciding to ask about it later. Mr. and Mrs. Cooper felt it was just Natalie's way of thanking Dr. Ramsey for saving her life. They would be very happy to have him as an honorary member of the family.

Mrs. Cooper raised her nose to the air and exclaimed, "Oh my! The oven! I have to check on my baking." She hurried to the kitchen and Christelle ran happily behind her.

Natalie turned to her father and softly said, "Papa, I have the best Christmas present I could ever wish for you."

"Having you back is the best Christmas present I could ever wish for."

"The second best then—and almost as wonderful. Well, yes and no. I can't imagine how dreadful it was for everyone, thinking I was dead. Well, then it is something almost as wonderful. Will you come with me?" she asked, taking him by the hand.

Natalie held out her other hand to her rescuer. "Dr. Ramsey, will you come with us for just a moment? I have something to show you." She led both men into the drawing room. Letting go of their hands, she hurried to the Christmas tree, blocking their view of it. The fragrance of her cherished Christmas tree filled the air around her. Slowly she moved aside and pointed to her father's special ornament. The look of astonishment on Dr. Ramsey's face was priceless. "I haven't seen that ornament in almost forty years," he said with reverence.

Before her father could respond, Natalie revealed, "Papa, Dr. Ramsey is your father and my grandfather."

She let the news sink in for a moment. "It worked, Papa. It worked! Your Star of Bethlehem ornament brought him back to you," she added with delight.

Both men turned to look at each other, searching for the past in each other's faces. Nathan Cooper saw immediately that they had the same eyes, and Dr. Ramsey's critical eye could see Evie throughout this man's countenance. With trembling arms, Dr. Ramsey embraced his son, which Nathan Cooper returned attempting to make up for forty lost years.

Dr. Ramsey went to the Christmas tree to look more closely at the ornament. Turning to his son, he asked, "May I?"

Mr. Cooper nodded. He came over and untied his beloved ornament and handed it to his father.

Holding the precious star in his hands, the years fell away. Dr. Ramsey found himself remembering his wife and their short life together and began to weep. He handed the ornament back to his son. "I will be able to tell you all about your mother and a family you've never known." Dr. Ramsey wiped his tears away and steeled himself for his next question. "May I ask, how is Mrs. Copper?"

"Mrs. Copper?" questioned Mr. Cooper.

"The woman who took you. She was your wet nurse."

"The woman who raised me was Amelia Cooper. She died when I was twenty years old. It was on her deathbed that I learned that she was not my mother. I kept her name because she was very good to me and I loved her very much. All these years I have been looking for a Mr. Victor Raimey as my father. I realize now that she had slurred your last name. Your name was the last words out of her mouth as she passed. But I would rather share our stories later. Right now I'm anxious to go and surprise my sweet wife. Care to come along so that I may properly present my father to her?"

"I would be honored."

To Natalie's delight, Mr. Cooper scooped her up and into his arms, just as he had done when she was a little girl, and carried her with him out of the room. Holding her tight he whispered, "I'm very happy that you have discovered my father, but most of all my heart is full of joy at having you home." He kissed her on the cheek and set her down before they entered the kitchen.

"I'm going to find Christelle. I don't want her to be alone," said Natalie, leaving her parents and grandfather to get acquainted.

❄ ❄ ❄

Sitting in the drawing room Natalie and Christelle couldn't get enough of each other. They shared some of the things that had happened while they were apart.

"Christelle, guess what?"

"What?"

"The man who saved me—Dr. Ramsey—is our grandfather!"

"He is? You mean we now have a grandfather?"

"Yes, a grandfather. He is Papa's father, so now we are going to get to know all about Papa's side of the family.

"That is really nice, isn't it?" said Christelle.

"Yes, it is!"

"Natalie, guess what?

"What?"

"It's your birthday."

"You're right! It is. I forgot all about it."

"Guess what else."

"What?"

"I placed the baby Jesus in the manger Christmas Eve and asked him to bring you home. And he did!"

"Yes, he did, and I am very, very happy to be home with you. Mama tells me that you never gave up hope that I would come home. Can you tell me why?"

"I never felt inside of me that you were gone."

"You didn't?" Natalie said, touched by her sister's faith.

"No—I was sure you would come home, and you did." Christelle scooted closer to Natalie so they were touching and could feel each other's warmth. "I made Mama and Papa put up your stocking. It has candy in it."

They were sharing the contents of Natalie's stocking when their father walked in. Natalie, feeling a little remorseful, said, "Papa, I lost my red bonnet!"

"No, it's not lost," he informed her. "Collin has it. He found it when we were out looking for you. He was so heartbroken that I haven't had the heart to ask for it."

Natalie let the word sink in: *heartbroken*. Collin must feel the same about her, as she does about him. *There's no time to waste,* she thought to herself. *I must go to him this very moment and set things right.*

"Collin must be in a dreadful state," she said out loud. "I need to go to him right now, Papa."

"Yes, you should indeed," he agreed.

Just then Natalie noticed that her Christmas presents had not been delivered. She looked to her father and he explained, "I never took the opportunity to deliver them to your friends. I felt that it would be too painful, so I decided to wait until later—maybe until after the New Year."

"I have some that I want to deliver now. They are for friends that we won't see at services, and after church will be too late. My bonnet and seeing Collin will have to wait a little longer. Once I see him, Papa, I won't be parted from him."

"I understand. I will go with you so I need to get ready. I'll be but a moment."

Natalie handed Christelle her Christmas stocking and whispered, "You can have whatever you want." She brushed Christelle's cheek in a show of affection and then got up from the sofa to go and get dressed for the cold.

Seeing Dr. Ramsey enter the room with petticoat tails in hand made her smile. She asked a question that had been on her mind while she had sat with Christelle. "Dr. Ramsey, what is your Christian name? I never thought to ask you while we were together."

"Victor Nathanial, which if memory serves me, is the reverse of your father's." He paused. "Natalie?"

"Yes, Grandfather?"

"I have Christmas. It's back here inside," he said patting his heart, "right where you wanted it."

"I am very happy. I couldn't possibly have a grandfather who didn't celebrate Christmas, so now I can keep you," she teased and then hugged him.

"Papa and I have some presents to deliver. Would you like to come with us, Grandfather?"

"Most assuredly," he said. "This is going to take some getting used to—being called Grandfather."

❋ ❋ ❋

Natalie, Mr. Cooper, and Dr. Ramsey went to deliver Natalie's Christmas gifts. At each home the two men stood side by side at the door and then Mr. Cooper knocked. When the recipient of the gift came to the door, the men stepped aside to reveal Natalie, and every time surprised gasps were surpassed by joy. Upon leaving each home, they had many Christmas wishes to carry with them.

As they came to the Bradley home Natalie said, "I am so nervous. My heart is beating so fast that I can't control it. I hope I don't faint; I am feeling lightheaded.

"Take some deep breaths and it will pass in a moment," counseled Dr. Ramsey.

Natalie complied, and after she started to feel better she said, "I'm not going to hide behind you. I can't wait that long."

❋ ❋ ❋

Christmas had come, and for Collin there was no joy in it. Memories of Natalie sent his heart into a deep abyss. He had a fixed, mournful, yearning gaze that saw nothing living. He chose to stay lost in his memories of her.

He found himself begging and bargaining with the Lord to bring her back to him, doing what so many others had done who had lost loved ones and couldn't bear it. "I promise that if you bring her back, I will . . ." A knock at the door interrupted him. Collin didn't want to answer it, but the rest of his family was at the back of the house enjoying breakfast, for which he had no appetite. Reluctantly he opened the door.

Collin's face was one of bewilderment. All he could do was look at her, fearing that she might dissolve at the slightest touch. Sinking to his knees, tears forming, he reached for her hand and held it to his cheek. Looking up at her, he asked, "How?"

Tenderly removing Collin's hand from hers, Natalie melted down and into Collins arms, where she answered in a tender whisper, "Remember the cabin on the other side of the hill from the mill? It belongs to Dr. Ramsey. He saved me," she said, nodding to the stranger.

Without turning to look at Dr. Ramsey, Collin murmured, "Thank you, thank you," over and over again, refusing to let go of her.

Natalie gently brushed the side of Collin's hair and brought them both up to their feet. She stepped back to see him. He appeared so very worn out and vulnerable that she pondered for a moment if she should carry out her plan. Deciding there should be no doubt in anyone's mind about her intentions, she chose to go ahead.

Collin never let her go with his eyes.

"Collin, I never got the chance to finish your Christmas present, so it will just have to wait." She reached for something near her heart and pulled out a little crumpled piece of mistletoe. "Papa, please hold this for me." She placed it in her father's hand and moved his hand high over Collin's head.

"This will give me the excuse for my impropriety." Whereupon she leaned forward, gently lifted Collin's face toward hers, and kissed him.

"Collin," she whispered, "I gave you this kiss with all my love, and I expect you to return it innumerable times." Then, looking at Collin with sparkling, mischievous eyes, she added, "Now, I do believe you have my red bonnet. I don't suppose that it looks very good on you. I would like it back, thank you."

Collin, still dazed from what just happened, turned, and flew through the house, yelling, "She's alive, she's alive! She kissed me, and she's alive!"

Soon he returned with the cherished bonnet. In his eyes shone the light that comes into the eyes of a man who has found love.

"Please take care and put it right back where it belongs," said Natalie. She lowered her head while Collin gently placed the bonnet over her brown tresses. Struggling with the bow, Collin turned the operation over to Natalie, who quickly finished tying her bonnet.

"Natalie, you're the most beautiful sight I've ever seen!" Collin whispered.

"Thank you, Collin. You've always been so very sweet to me."

Natalie was looking at Collin and forward to a life with him. She cherished him and was never going to let him forget it.

"I hesitate to interrupt," said Mrs. Cooper, who had arrived with Christelle just in time to witness the kiss, "but we need to get on over to the church. Christmas services are about to start, and we have many more people with whom to share this miracle."

With that, the joyous group made their way through town. Distant sounds of carols greeted them as they headed for the church. Natalie and a beaming Collin walked hand in hand. They were followed by Mr. Cooper, who had Mrs. Cooper and Christelle on his right and Dr. Ramsey—his newfound father—on his left.

Mr. Cooper called to his daughter. "Natalie, how on earth are you going to make next Christmas better than this one?"

She leaned back, and with a wink to her father, she whispered, "I have an idea Papa, but it will take Mr. Bradley's help."

"Daughter, you never cease to surprise me. Let's let time decide, shall we?"

❄ ❄ ❄

The street was transforming in the morning sunshine, it glistened like sugar icing with dark ribbons where sleighs had passed through.

A small, white dog they knew as Tippy barked ecstatically while stirring up a flurry of snow. Now and again he disappeared under the snow and reappeared with head up and tail wagging before dashing off again under it. The snow was pure delight for the little rascal.

Noticing the party of passersby, Tippy ran directly for them, bouncing first off Collin, then Mr. Cooper, and so on, making sure that he gave everyone in the party a proper Christmas greeting. With happy barking he raced in fierce tight circles around them. After making sure that everyone had Tippyfied greetings at least twice, he sat himself down, creating a fan in the snow with his wagging tail and looking very much pleased with himself.

As the happy party crossed the threshold of the church, they could hear Bishop Versey speaking, and they paused.

"Brothers and sisters, it was Natalie Cooper's desire to read the Christmas story in Luke to us this year. I dearly wish she were here to read it for us. I'm very sorry, I admit, that there were some who were not in favor of her doing it. I only wish that I had been stronger in my convictions. The story of the Nativity in Luke is why we have Christmas. It is for Christ that we all come together, and that is why we are here. . . . I will now begin the reading.

"'And she brought forth her firstborn son, and wrapped him in swaddling clothes, and laid him in a manger; because there was no room for them in the inn. . . .'"

The back of the congregation was the first to notice the Coopers arrive. Murmurs began to ripple through the pews. Natalie knew there was no good time to interrupt, so she moved forward with Collin down the aisle. The ripple turned into a wave of exclamations. Everyone knew that they were witnessing something extraordinary. Wonder and delight interspersed with sobs reached Bishop Versey, and he looked up from his reading.

On the bishop's face, the dignity of his office and the joy of the moment fought for mastery. Not believing his own eyes, he said without being able to stop himself, "Oh, dear Lord, a miracle!" Then, remembering another scripture in Luke, he said directly to the Cooper family, "For with God nothing shall be impossible." Smiles and tears abounded everywhere he looked.

Bishop Versey motioned Natalie to come up and stand by him. He settled down the jubilant congregation and asked in the perfect stillness, "How is this possible?"

Looking around, Natalie found herself in the midst of those who loved her. She explained as briefly as she could: "I fell and struck my head and nearly drowned. Dr. Ramsey saved me, and the snowstorms made it impossible for him to get me home until this very morning."

Joy filled every nook and cranny of that little white church. In the hearts of every man, woman, and child who were blessed to witness this Christmas Day miracle—of one who was thought lost and had now returned—burned feelings of renewed hope and the blessings of their Savior.

Bishop Versey whispered to Natalie, "Shall we do this?" And with perfect timing they delivered the Nativity together with one voice.

Mrs. Messing wept.